A Healthy Way To Die

LIONEL BLACK

AVON
PUBLISHERS OF BARD, CAMELOT AND DISCUS BOOKS

AVON BOOKS
A division of
The Hearst Corporation
959 Eighth Avenue
New York, New York 10019
Copyright © 1976 by Lionel Black
Published by arrangement with the author.
Library of Congress Catalog Card Number: 78-70867
ISBN: 0-380-43661-2

All rights reserved, which includes the right
to reproduce this book or portions thereof in
any form whatsoever. For information address
Avon Books.

First Avon Printing, April, 1979

AVON TRADEMARK REG. U.S. PAT. OFF. AND IN
OTHER COUNTRIES, MARCA REGISTRADA,
HECHO EN U.S.A.

Printed in the U.S.A.

STARVING TO DEATH

The Hostess
For her, the fat farm used to mean the fat life. Now she was suddenly out of a job.

The Singer
Today she was a guest at Gorsedene. Tomorrow she might be an inmate in jail.

The Columnist
Usually he had the goods on everybody else. This time he was the target of blackmail—aimed at his most sensitive spot.

The Beauty
It was more than a mother's love that made her fight for her child.

The Tycoon
He loved money, women, and scandal, in that order. Death came to him swiftly, violently—and very suspiciously.

Kate and Henry Theobald knew something sinister was happening, particularly when the man's death rocked the Stock Exchange and threatened an international financial crash. Gradually they discovered one patient after another with different reasons for wanting the man dead. Then violence exploded again . . .

Other Avon books by
Lionel Black

DEATH BY HOAX   41376 $1.75

A Healthy Way To Die

CHAPTER 1

"IT'S A lovely assignment," said Kate Theobald to her husband. "A week at Gorsedene. Every woman's dream."

"I'd sooner you than me."

"That smoked salmon was delicious, Henry darling. Was it frantically expensive?"

They were dining at their favourite little restaurant in Chelsea, the one they were careful not to talk about to their friends. The ambience was, of course, rough-peasant, but the food was something.

"Outrageously."

"Ah well, you won't have to feed me for a week. Come to that, nobody will."

He smiled. "What do they charge? More than one hundred pounds a week, isn't it, for starving you on one grapefruit daily, and unlimited boiled water? I think I'd almost sooner go to gaol than to a health farm."

"But you have that irritating metabolism that doesn't put on an ounce, no matter what you eat. Whereas I . . . There's no need to grin, Henry."

The waiter arrived with the main dishes. "The steak and kidney pudding?" he asked.

"For madam," said Henry. "The dover sole for me."

"Well, it's my last fling," Kate defended. "And I adore steak and kidney pudding. And since I'm going to lose so much weight, I may as well have a little more to lose, to get my money's worth, or rather, their money's worth."

"You newspaper people! You live on the fat of the land. But perhaps that isn't quite apt."

"Butch called me over to the news desk, and said there's this invitation for a reporter to spend a week at Gorsedene, and he couldn't think of anyone more suitable to send

7

than I—the pig. A little more of the gravy, please, and perhaps just a morsel more of the crust. Thank you. Then he made some offensive remark about saving me the expense of a new girdle. Your fish all right, darling?"

"Excellent. Just pink on the bone."

"I read up Gorsedene in the office clippings library. By the vast publicity they've had, I imagine they ask a couple of journalists down for free every month. Still, I suppose all it really costs them is half-a-dozen grapefruit and a few slices of lemon.

"The place itself is fabulously luxurious, except for the food, of course. Beautifully furnished rooms, colour television in every nook and cranny, servants rushing in at the slightest touch on the bell, a private golf course, vast swimming pool, saunas by the dozen, wonderful massage all day long if you like. Heaven! They throw in yoga classes at no extra cost, but you have to bring your own leotard.

"All the great and famous seem to go there—American movie stars by the planeload, Arab sheikhs dripping with oil, business millionaires drying out, fashionable playwrights, and all the jet-set women. The car park is crammed with Rolls and Bentleys, but the wealthiest arrive by helicopter—there's a helicopter pad on the lawn. I suppose that gives the sort of cachet one got by arriving anywhere in a motor car in about 1905."

"Will you be expected to write much?"

"What I have in mind is a sort of amusing little piece for the women's page, and perhaps a couple of pars for the gossip column. May I have another glass of this excellent claret, darling? We shan't need another bottle, shall we?"

"I hope not," he said, "the price it is."

Kate was reaching for the menu. "Something rather simple for a sweet, don't you think? Chocolate profiteroles?"

"And, after that, a whacking great wedge of Stilton?"

"Oh no," she said reprovingly. "Just coffee. And perhaps a touch of Armagnac to go with it?"

Back at home—rather a cramped little flat, only two rooms, kitchen and bath, and all those damned stairs to walk up; but beautifully placed, just off the King's Road

—she called to him from the bathroom. She had stripped and was standing on the bathroom scales.

"I need a witness to exactly how much weight I'm going to lose."

Henry crouched to squint at the scale's register. "Stand still," he said. "Don't sway about. It alters the reading. That's better. One hundred and forty-two pounds. What's that? Ten stone two."

Kate squealed. "It can't be."

He looked up at her, amused. "Even Butch had noticed."

"Don't be a cad, darling. Anyway, it doesn't matter. Think what a wonderful figure I'm going to have in a week's time."

He stood up and gently squeezed her bottom.

"It's not too bad now, if you ask me," he said, "particularly for bed."

"Oh Henry darling, can we possibly, after that huge meal? Shan't we get indigestion or something?"

"If you're going to desert me for a week..."

She put her arms round his neck. "I suppose we ought to try."

Much later, at some time in the small hours, he was woken by the sound of the bedroom door. He switched on the bedside lamp. Kate, still naked, was returning to the room.

"Where have you been?"

"Just getting myself a little snack," she confessed. "Only a couple of sausages from the fridge. Well, you know how hungry sex always makes me, darling."

CHAPTER 2

THE MID-SEPTEMBER SUN was shining warmly when she arrived at lunch-time on Sunday. Lunch-time, she thought sadly. All she had been offered was half a grapefruit with no sugar, and a glass of boiled water flavoured with a slice of either lemon or orange; the choice was hers.

Gorsedene itself was magnificent. The main house was obviously late eighteenth or early nineteenth century, with a fine Georgian front and some ridiculously large number of rooms. The entrance hall rose through two storeys, with the ceiling supported by carved and painted pillars, and with a lovely central staircase curving away to the right. The reception desk stood beneath it. The receptionist taking Kate's registration asked what newspapers she would like.

"None. I'm having a holiday from that."

The receptionist looked up in surprise, then smiled tolerantly. "Oh, of course. You're the newspaper reporter." She nodded to the porter who had carried in Kate's luggage. "Mrs. Theobald is in Room Twelve."

Henry, who had driven Kate there, walked with her up the stairs behind the porter. He was an Indian, of grace, intelligent features, wearing a white jacket buttoned up to his neck, and white trousers; quite a young man, probably a student working through his vacation, Kate guessed. When they reached her room, Henry tipped him lavishly. The Indian took that as a matter of routine.

Kate gazed appreciatively at the room. It was large, charmingly furnished. A bowl of roses stood on the side table, a television in the corner. The door in the inner wall led into a pink-tiled shower-room.

Henry, who had wandered to the window and lifted

aside the white nylon drapes, called to her to come and see. "Lush, eh?"

Kate's room was in the main building, the original mansion, but at the back. It looked into a quadrangle, along the other three sides of which had been built new blocks of rooms, brightly panelled, with large windows, some with balconies on which patients were lying in chaises-longues in the sun.

The centre of the quadrangle was occupied by a pale-blue swimming pool of considerable size, surrounded by tiled paving dotted with brightly-cushioned basketwork chairs, coloured parasols, gleaming white tables; around the edges, Italian terracotta pots crammed with petunias, roses, geraniums, fuchsias, spikey cactus shapes, and the greens and whites of variegated trailing plants.

Several of the chairs were filled with women in bikinis and floppy straw hats, and a couple of men were swimming slowly in the pool.

"Could be the front cover of a travel agent's brochure," Henry murmured. "Well, enjoy yourself, darling. I must back my old Jag rather shamefacedly out of the car park; all those Rolls and Bentleys! Quite humbling."

"Ring me now and then," she said. "What will you do with yourself?"

"I've a couple of briefs to gen up on, for when the Michaelmas term starts. Then, of course, I shall look up some of my old girl-friends." He grinned. "And I shall eat at my club."

"I can't think why I love you," she sighed.

Not long after he had gone there was a tap at her door. The woman who came in was youngish. A few years ago she must have been quite lovely. Now there were slight signs of slackening round the throat and mouth, the cosmetics were a little too thick, the hips starting to plump. But still a beauty—and well aware of it, Kate thought.

"Good afternoon, Mrs. Theobald, and welcome to Gorsedene. I'm Janet Dimpsey. My husband's the director. I always have to do duty on Sundays—staff problems, you know. We suffer dreadfully from them in this remote place."

"It looks marvellous."

"Well, thank you. I hope you enjoy your stay. You haven't, of course, come for health reasons. But if you would like to take the normal treatment . . . "

"Yes, please. I got on the bathroom scales last night. Quite shattering."

Janet Dimpsey smiled. "Then if you'll just get into a nightdress and dressing-gown—that's the Gorsedene uniform, Mrs. Theobald—I'll take you along to my husband for a preliminary consultation."

The director's rooms were on the first floor, near the entrance staircase. A small boy was playing with a toy truck in the anteroom.

"This is Christopher," Mrs. Dimpsey told Kate, "my infant."

"You live here in the main house?"

"No. We have a cottage in the grounds. You may have noticed it as you came up the drive, on the right, facing the river bank."

Kate nodded. "It looks charming."

"It's a pleasant cottage, and mercifully small. Staff problems again. On Sundays, when I come over here on duty, I have to bring Christopher, for I've nobody to leave him with at home."

The door of the consulting-room opened and the director showed out a fair-haired woman in the regulation dressing-gown and nightdress.

"Mrs. Sadler starts a course of treatment tomorrow morning," he said to his wife. "I'll give you the details for the book later. And now I'm to meet . . . ?"

"Mrs. Theobald, our guest from the *Daily Post*."

"Ah yes, of course," he said. "How good of you to come, Mrs. Theobald. Will you step in, please?"

The consulting-room was large, pleasant, the big windows looking out across the front lawns to the footbridge over the river. The walls were hung with paintings, mostly vivid and contemporary. The carpet was thick.

The director asked Kate to be seated in front of his wide mahogany desk, the leather top piled with papers. He himself went round to his rotating desk chair.

Pelham Dimpsey was a tall, thin man in a white medical

overall, with a long, serious-looking face, high forehead and thick brown hair backing from the temples.

He started to tell her of the aims and attitudes of a health farm, "as it is popularly called, Mrs. Theobald." He smiled politely. He seemed an immensely polite man, but with a slightly nervous manner, she thought. "I myself think of it as a therapeutic establishment, a retreat in which we live naturally for a brief time. Oh, how we maltreat our bodies, Mrs. Theobald . . . !"

As he went on about the marvels of the human body in its natural state, and the benefits of a dietetic approach to life, he seemed to take on almost religious intensity. Kate nodded appreciatively now and then, which was apparently all that he required.

His facial skin, she noticed, was very clear and smooth, almost transparent. The whites of his pale blue eyes were of a detergent-ad whiter-than-whiteness. The backs of his long, tendon-thin hands, busy now preparing a medical-history sheet for her, were thickly clad with brown hair, and the fingers were tufted.

He was asking about her previous illnesses. The usual childish complaints, of course, and removal of the appendix. Once, years ago, a vexatious month of glandular fever. He raised his thick brown eyebrows sympathetically as he noted that. Any rheumatism? An occasional touch of the screws, she admitted. Indigestion? Well, now and then; a newspaper life makes demands on the digestion. He nodded understandingly and began to probe delicately into such matters as bowel movements and menstrual problems. No children of the marriage? No, replied Kate firmly.

"Now then," he said, laying down his pen, "let us see how you fare on the scales."

"The moment of truth," she murmured, taking off her dressing-gown and stepping on to the scales that stood against the wall.

Pelham Dimpsey smiled dutifully as he carefully adjusted the weights on the arm of the scale. Kate saw that he was concealing his boredom. How often must he have heard every possible comic remark about overweight women!

"Ten stone, two pounds and three ounces," he noted.

"What should it be?"

"At your age, height, and build, Mrs. Theobald," he assessed, looking at her studiously, "you would be happier at nine and a half stone."

"Happier indeed," she fervently agreed.

2

Back in her room, Kate looked out of the window at the pool, around which several more patients had gathered. She put on a sunbathing dress and went down.

It was a lazy scene. The half-dozen people in the pool were floating idly on their backs, or occasionally turning to swim a few gentle strokes. Those in the basket chairs were mostly motionless, eyes closed behind sunglasses, skins carefully oiled, and women's noses covered by little white protectors.

She saw the woman who had preceded her with Dimpsey sitting by herself at one of the tables, the other chair unoccupied. Kate strolled over and smiled. "Isn't this super? Everybody so relaxed and restful."

"None of them has the strength to be anything else."

Kate grinned and took the unoccupied chair. "May I?"

"Of course. We met in Dimpsey's anteroom, didn't we? I'm Phoebe Sadler."

"Kate Theobald. I'm here on rather false pretences. I work on a newspaper—the *Daily Post*—and I've come to write an article."

"You're lucky. They'll let you eat."

"Oh no," Kate assured her. "I'm to take the cure properly—for personal as well as professional reasons."

Phoebe Sadler grimaced. "You'll regret it. It's hell."

"You've been here before?"

"Several times. I don't know why I keep on coming back for punishment. Just masochism, I suppose."

A man emerging from the pool nodded to her as he walked past, and said morosely, "There's nothing the matter with me that a pint of bitter beer wouldn't cure."

"You'll notice," said Phoebe to Kate, "that almost the

sole subjects of conversation in this place are either food or drink."

Kate smiled and they lapsed into silence. Phoebe Sadler, she mused, was another slightly faded beauty; the fair skin of a honey blonde, a slim figure, the breasts starting to droop, but wonderful legs. She had pressed out her cigarette, put on sunglasses, and lain back in the chair dozing. She looked tired. As her face relaxed there were little signs of strain around the mouth and at the corners of the eyes. Walk half a mile along King's Road and you would see a dozen women like her—smart, attractive, dissatisfied, bitchy.

Kate closed her eyes. It was pleasant in the sun. She was on the edge of sleep when a shadow across her face disturbed her. A man and a woman were standing by the table. Phoebe Sadler was just rousing to greet them.

"Well, hallo. Are you going to swim?"

"Mary is," he said. He had that pleasantest of all American accents, the cultivated tones of Boston. "I'm just going to sit right here in this unexpected sun. By your national radio forecast this morning, it ought to be raining. But then, that's the only invariable truth about English weather—whatever you hear about it turns out to be a lie."

"Pull up some chairs. Here's another newspaper person. Mrs. Theobald. She writes for the *Daily Post*."

"And you?" asked Kate.

"My stuff is mostly syndicated. My name's Michael Neal."

"The columnist?"

He chuckled agreeably. "That's the nicest thing has happened to me in years. Did you hear that, Mary? This is my wife, Mary. Here's this charming English newspaperwoman, Mrs. Theobald . . . "

"Kate."

"Here's this charming Kate Theobald, and I meet her three thousand miles from Washington, and she has actually heard of me."

"There can't be a newspaper writer anywhere who hasn't," said Kate. "Come to that, there can't be many intelligent newspaper readers who haven't."

"You're my favorite Englishwoman," he told her.

And he might qualify, she thought, as her idea of her favourite American. He was a burly, broad-framed man of middle years, not handsome, but with a friendly, perceptive look, quiet, yet powerful. His column was certainly one of the three or four most respected in world journalism (since he had Washington, one could say, sewn up), and immensely influential because of the man's notable integrity. The wife—dark-haired, olive-skinned, slight of figure—was younger.

The wife got up and shed her bathing wrap. "I'll leave you to your idle chatter," she said. She had a more clipped accent than he. It was probably New York, Kate surmised, or possibly Middle West; she was not expert at American accents. "I'm going to swim."

She had an enviably neat little body, and moved like a dancer. From his glance, it was obvious that her husband doted. The old man's darling. But Kate hastily reproved herself; he was not at all old, just splendidly mature.

When he had watched her dive trimly into the pool, Michael Neal turned around again, smiling happily.

"Your wife certainly doesn't need to slim," said Kate.

"She thinks she does. Even a pound excess, she says, makes her look plump. As for me—" he patted his stomach —"years of extravagant living. Still, in only three days I've lost five pounds already. This is a wonderful place, don't you think?"

"I've only just arrived."

"Oh, you're in for a real experience. You British always make out that you're so old-fashioned and inept—and we understand that you're secretly smiling at us barbarians as you do so. But I don't know of any health farm in the States with more modern equipment than there is here—underwater massage, every sort of machine for rheumatism and arthritis, diagnostic machines, saunas, steam baths, colonic lavage, everything. And you've got such expert operators. Osteopaths, physiotherapists, masseurs, the lot. There's a man massages me—I thought he'd actually broken my back when I got off the table. A couple of hours later I felt ten years younger."

"It ought to be good," said Kate, "the amount they charge."

"My dear Kate, it may seem costly to you. But to us it's wonderfully cheap, compared with what this sort of place charges in the States. My sister, who lives in Los Angeles, comes here for a fortnight every spring. Including the air fare, it costs her about twenty per cent less than a fortnight in an equivalent health farm in California. Of course, the currency exchange favours us, but not so much as it did."

"I must have a look around this bargain," said Kate, getting up, "before I get too feeble to walk anywhere."

"Let's talk later. It's great to meet somebody from Fleet Street. I live in such a claustrophobic, over-heated, self-important little circuit, called Washington DC, that it's wonderful to hear something from the real world."

"See you at the next serving of grapefruit."

3

She wandered past the pool and through the archway under the rear line of buildings. To the right lay the voluptuous car park, and beyond it the riding stables—a cobbled yard, a rectangle of stalls with grain stores above. Two men were hoisting heavy sacks from a truck up to the open door of the store, where a third man was heaving them in.

She looked into a tall wooden building next to the car park. There were two squash courts, neither in use. The corridor alongside led to a gymnasium, full of gear. A girl in shirt and shorts was hauling herself slowly into acrobatics on the rope handles. At the far end two men in fencing masks were practising with foils.

Kate tried the door at the end of a branching corridor. It opened on to a billiards room. One man was bent over the table to make his stroke. He and the three other players looked up irritably.

"Sorry," Kate apologized, backing out; billiards is no affair of women.

She left the sports building and took the path away from the car park. It led, through a gate in a yew hedge, to a large vegetable garden, excellently tended, growing mostly salad crops, with a row of greenhouses stuffed with tomatoes. The windows of the building that the vegetable garden adjoined were those of the Gorsedene kitchens. Curious, Kate walked towards them; what on earth did Gorsedene want with kitchens? But she knew, of course, that the place boasted a dining-room, and that guests who were there to unwind, or dry out, rather than lose weight, could eat regular, health-giving meals.

Two girls were preparing massive bowls of green salad. On one wall was fixed a row of electric urns, like samovars, doubtless boiling the staple diet of water. She recalled from the clippings that the place made its own yoghurt—probably in several huge earthenware basins on a far counter, covered with damp cloths. A man in a white apron and chef's cap—ultimate irony—was inserting trays of jacket potatoes into the electric ovens.

Kate turned away hastily from this gastronomic spectacle. She traversed the vegetable garden and emerged on to the Gorsedene golf course; only nine holes, the brochure shamefacedly admitted. But it was mercifully flat. Several pairs and fours were striking their way round it. Their pace seemed leisurely.

As she turned aside from the links and started back towards the main building, there was a whirr from the sky. A helicopter. A patient arriving in the grand manner. That, she guessed, did not often happen. She must see it. So she made for the terrace fronting the old mansion where the helicopter pad was set in the lawn midway from the house to the river bank.

The terrace was scattered with parasols, chairs and tables, most of them now occupied, since the Indian porter was emerging with trays of tea. Even the most rigid dieter was allowed an afternoon cup of tea, preferably with lemon, permissibly with milk, but never any sugar and, of course, unaccompanied by food.

Kate reached the terrace just as the circling helicopter was descending towards the pad. Pelham Dimpsey came out of the house and gestured to the Indian to put down his tray and follow him on to the lawn to meet the arrival.

The Americans, Michael Neal and his wife, were seated at a table near to where Kate was standing, and Michael called to her to join them.

"This place isn't so flush with excitement that one can afford to miss a VIP entrance," he said.

The helicopter put down, the engine cut, the rotors gradually slowed. The first to emerge was a thin man in a dark suit. He stood aside to make way for a tall, fair-haired man whom Pelham Dimpsey went forward to greet and to lead across the lawn into the house. The thin man waited behind to receive a rawhide suitcase and several document wallets which the pilot handed from the machine. He passed them on to the Indian, who preceded him into the entrance. A few minutes later the pilot, a sturdy young man in jeans and a highneck sweater, clambered from his helicopter and followed them.

"The VIP," murmured Michael.

"But I know him," said Kate. "I interviewed him once. He's Philip Antrobus."

"Yes, the financier."

Kate was a little puzzled. Michael seemed to be compelling himself to speak, as though it were a sudden strain, a difficulty. Mary had turned her head away and was looking towards the river.

"You know him?" asked Kate.

"Know of him. He has American interests, as well as British."

"The last news suggested that he'd caught a cold in the States, didn't it?" asked Kate, trying to remember. "Something to do with a big gamble that failed."

Michael shook his head. "A defence contract. But it hasn't failed yet. There's been a lot of dispute about it in Washington, but so far no decision."

"He's said to be fabulously rich," Kate went on. She could not help wondering why Mary Neal was still keeping her head turned away from them; but probably she was simply uninterested. "He was one of the City whizz-kids of the 'sixties, when the great boom was on, and half-a-dozen youngsters backed by mushroom banking firms made impudent takeover bids that suddenly turned out to be for real. They all ran up millionaire fortunes in a few years. But most of them lost it all again, usually by wild property speculations at high interest rates just before the market collapsed. However, Philip Antrobus didn't lose. I heard in the office the other day that he's one of the few to come through the slump with probably more than he had before. Except for this American thing, they said."

"Could be. Don't forget that we went into recession too. Ah, now we get some tea. Over here, Charan?"

The Indian had returned with a fresh trayload. He heard Michael Neal and came across, smiling gravely.

"Kate, this is Charan Lal, the one man it's vital to know, isn't that so, Charan?" said Michael. "He's the most important member of the establishment, the keystone of the arch."

The Indian smiled politely. "If you say so, Mr. Neal." He had an educated voice, and not much of the singsong Indian lilt. "Good afternoon, madam. Tea with milk?"

"With lemon," said Kate. "I'm a good-conduct prisoner."

"That won't earn you any remission," Michael assured her. "Milk for me, Charan. There's nourishment in milk. How about you, darling?"

"Lemon," replied his wife. Now that she had turned to face them again her look was calm; but Kate had the odd impression that she had had to struggle to make it so.

When Lal had served the tea and moved on, Michael said, "He's a fine boy, that. One could say that the true hope for India, and maybe for much of Asia, lies in him and his kind. He comes from a desperately poor family working on a tea plantation in Assam. One of your missionaries gave him a start at learning, and he ran his way up to college in Calcutta. Now he's over here at one of your universities, I forget just which, studying economics and law, and I'll wager he'll take a fine honours degree, and go home to help run his country."

"And I'll wager you're the only man here who has talked to him about himself."

"He's one worth talking to. I can always tell, can't you? But of course you can. You're a newspaperwoman—or, as we have to say in these days of female emancipation, a newspaper person. The sexes must equate."

Kate laughed. "I'd love to hear you tell that to my husband."

"Is he here?"

"Not Henry. At this moment he'll be sitting in some Chelsea café, sipping China tea and nibbling a cream cake. This evening he'll settle to a huge dinner at his club, and a half-bottle of claret with it. Henry never puts on an ounce in weight—which isn't why I love him."

"Is he a newspaperman—sorry, person?"

"No, he's a barrister, a lawyer. Very respectable and proper, rather conservative, fairly handsome—and quite a dear."

"Do I ever get that sort of testimonial from you?" Michael asked his wife.

"As if I would tell you. You're conceited enough already."

"I'm starting to feel really hungry," said Kate. "When do we get anything to eat?"

"Dinner-time," he replied. "We each get half an unsweetened grapefruit."

"Nothing more?"

"Not until breakfast tomorrow—that's another half-grapefruit. But before dinner there's the cocktail hour."

"You can't mean it."

He laughed. "At six o'clock we all gather in the big lounge back there, overlooking this terrace. Then you can have a cocktail of boiled water flavoured with either lemon or orange slices. And there's a standard joke it's obligatory to laugh at. You'd better be warned. Somebody will ask you whether you'll take the Dry Martini or the Bronx. Then you laugh like a mocking-bird."

Kate promised to try, though it would come hard.

The pilot of the helicopter and the thin man who had arrived with Philip Antrobus—probably his secretary—emerged from the house and walked over to the machine. All the people on the terrace watched lazily as they clambered in, the rotors started and, after a few minutes, the thing lifted and sped away.

"They'll be eating a satisfying meal someplace," mused Michael, "about the time we sit down to our half-grapefruit."

"I don't actually wish them any harm," said Kate thoughtfully, "but why does even a brief experience of hunger make one feel so vindictive?"

"Homo sapiens," he said. "Hunger strips the veneer and you get down to the nature of the beast."

"I wish I loved the human race," she quoted sadly. "How does one pass the time in this place? What happens after the grapefruit? How does one get through the rest of the evening?"

Some people make up fours of bridge, he told her. Some read. Most go to their rooms and lie on their beds, watching television in a semi-daze.

"Is television obligatory too?" she asked. "Is it Big Brother stuff?"

"Oh no. You can always shut that off—if you're not too exhausted to rise from your bed and turn the switch."

Kate sighed. "I'll probably have to watch the damned screen until midnight. I'm exhausted already."

CHAPTER 3

THE FULL REGIMEN began on Monday morning. Soon after the maid delivered the breakfast half-grapefruit and silver pot of boiled water to Kate's bedroom, and while she was still lying in bed, Janet Dimpsey arrived with her timetable.

"I've put you down for a steam bath at ten o'clock, Mrs. Theobald, followed by massage. Your masseuse is named Norah. If you prefer, I can arrange for a male masseur, but they're all rather booked for the next few mornings."

"Leave me with Norah. I don't think Henry would approve of a male. How about underwater massage?"

"Not for the first two days, I suggest. It's a strenuous, exhausting treatment. Some people can't stand it at all. If you like to try it on, say, Wednesday? All right, I'll put you down for that morning at eleven. But if you find it too exhausting, I do urge you to say so, and not repeat it."

"Trust me," Kate assured her.

"Now, physiotherapy. I see from my husband's notes that you occasionally suffer from lumbar pain, suggesting, of course, some rheumatic trouble in the spine. I think the steam baths and massage may be sufficient to break that up, but I'd like Mrs. Norman to have a look at you. She's our senior physiotherapist, and fully qualified, of course. I've made an appointment with her for twelve noon today."

"Thank you. Does that complete it?"

Janet Dimpsey nodded. "Treatment is all in the mornings. The afternoons are free, and most patients use them for relaxation—a walk in the surrounding countryside, perhaps, or hacking if you prefer. There's a riding stable at the rear of the buildings. The hire of a hack is, of course, an extra.

"Alternatively, there's the golf course—only nine holes, but we had no space for a full-size links—or the pool, or tennis. On the noticeboard in the entrance hall there's a tennis list. If you put your name on it, you'll be invited to take part in a doubles. Later in the afternoon there are yoga classes in the gymnasium. I can put you down for those if you wish. I take it you have brought a track suit or leotard."

"Actually, not. I'm not much of an enthusiast for yoga. I'll make it the pool, and perhaps a walk if I'm feeling strong enough by then."

Janet Dimpsey smiled, but only faintly. She seemed, Kate thought, depressed, compared with her cheerful manner the previous afternoon. She wondered whether the woman had been crying. There was slight redness round her eyes; but probably the cosmetics were not so carefully applied on a working morning.

"Where do I go for treatment?" Kate asked.

"To the lower ground floor. The treatment rooms are well signposted. The usual thing, by the way, is simply to put on a dressing-gown over your nightdress and not to get dressed until the treatment is finished for the day."

When Kate started to go down, indeed, the first man she bumped into—almost literally, as he came out of the door of the next room to hers—was wearing a resplendent Chinese silken gown embroidered with a huge dragon.

She saw at once who it was.

"Good morning, Mr. Antrobus. Actually, we have met. I'm Kate Theobald. I interviewed you for the *Post* a couple of years ago. But I don't suppose you remember."

"Of course I do," he answered vaguely.

He was still handsome, though he must by now be around forty. There were surprisingly few signs of his notorious dissipation, all that womanizing, all those scandals; there was scarcely a gossip column anywhere in the mid-sixties without a salacious paragraph or two about Philip Antrobus and his latest pick-up. He had brought a couple of libel suits, she recalled, winning one (though with derisory damages) and settling the other out of court.

"That was a charming article you wrote about me," he said. "Much too flattering."

So, of course, he had not remembered her at all. She had written mischievously, and the office lawyer had had doubts, and made her rewrite parts of it.

"But excuse me," he said. "I've forgotten something."

And he went back into the room.

"Typical millionaire's brush-off," Kate murmured to herself as she wandered down the stairs. "I ought to have a sexier dressing-gown."

The lounges and corridors were full of patients in their nightclothes, looking frowzy; the men neater than the women. She saw the Neals in the crowd and waved to them, but had no time for talk. Her steam-bath appointment was almost due.

Wide stairs led down to what must have been the cellars of the original mansion, but were now gleaming with white paint and frosted panels, glowing with hidden striplights, and alive with patients preparing for treatment.

The steam bath-house, a large room, was lined with cabinets, in each of which sat a woman, only her head protruding.

"Mrs. Theobald?" asked the girl in charge. A cheerful girl in white short-sleeved overall buttoned down the front, white socks and gumshoes. "Good morning, madam. I'm Phyllis."

She opened an empty cabinet and settled Kate on the white stool inside, closed the door over her so that only her head was free, and turned on the steam. "Let me know at once if you feel it's getting too hot, Mrs. Theobald. After the bath, I'll pass you on to Norah for massage, in the cubicle next door."

The women's faces sticking out from the cabinets around the room all looked content. Hot though it was, the steam bath was pleasantly relaxing. Kath found herself relishing the idea of sweat rolling a few ounces of fat off her body inside the contraption, as it was soon streaming in runnels down her face and neck.

She looked around, smiling at all those female heads gossiping to each other.

The head next to hers was florid-faced, with long dark hair twisted into a knot to top; and somehow familiar.

The head smiled back. "Great, ain't it? Cleans up the skin lovely. Dirt oozes out. You may think there isn't any, but you wait until Phyllis takes you out, luv."

Kate was trying to place her. She must be showbiz. She tried fixing a mental rectangle round the face, and at once got it—the pop singer with that awful hour on BBC One.

"You're Bella."

" 'Sright."

She looked more like a suburban housewife than the crude, promiscuous little bit she was reputed to be. She chattered cheerfully to Kate, rattling out stories of Gorsedene, of the people she had met there, of the people who worked there. Her voice, deprived of a microphone held an inch from her lips, was merely a Midlands backstreet whine. She might have been a Birmingham housewife chatting to her neighbour over the garden fence. It was Birmingham she came from, Kate recalled. She had been heard and promoted by a disc jockey having a night out in some sleazy joint where she sang when the customers tired of the record-player, and bedded down with the proprietor and his mates when the customers had gone.

When Phyllis got her out of the steam bath, Kate noticed with amusement the sag of the unsupported belly and the plumpness of the hips she shook so profitably in front of the cameras.

"See you after massage," said Bella, wrapping a towel round herself. "You having Norah? That's good, I always have Norah. She's the best. Gives you bleeding hell."

Which was right enough, Kate found, when she was released from the steam bath, wrapped in a towel, and despatched to the neighbouring cubicle for massage. Norah was a burly woman. When she got down to the base of the spine, the patient knew it. Kate tried holding her breath, then grunting. Grunting helped.

In an interval she remarked, "Plenty to say for herself, the pop singer."

Norah nodded. "But she's a good sort. I've been massaging her regularly for four years—she comes here three times every year. If she didn't she'd be enormous. She brought her mother once—about five feet tall, and well over one hundred pounds. Ethel has the same build."

"Ethel?"

"Bella's just the name she sings by. Ethel Spicer she is really. There now, that'll do for the first treatment. Now you're to see Mrs. Norman. Second door on the left along the corridor. She won't find much wrong with you."

Nor did she. Mrs. Norman, a tough little Scot, told her to strip and walk about the room, turning this way and that, then bend backwards, forwards, sideways. Kate was uncomfortably aware that she was going red in the face. Then Mrs. Norman got her on the table and prodded her spine.

"Tension down there, Mrs. Theobald. You must be loosened up a wee mite. But the steam baths and massage should free that in a few days. You don't need physiotherapy."

"Underwater massage?" asked Kate.

The idea of that machine intrigued her—lying in a warm bath and being pummelled hydraulically.

Mrs. Norman shrugged. "If you like. It willna' harm you. But leave it a couple of days yet. It's drastic."

2

By afternoon Kate felt that the whole regimen was more than drastic. It was sheer cruelty, almost sadism.

Occasionally she chided herself. Only twenty-four hours of hunger and she was whining with self-pity. Millions in the Third World were hungry month after month, year after year. She should be fraught with compassion. She tried to feel compassionate for all those poor, hungry millions, but then her thoughts wandered and she caught herself planning the dinner Henry would buy her the evening she got out of this hell-hole. It was shaming.

Yet the effects of even so short a period of hunger were startling. She started to read a book, but desisted after a couple of pages. She felt a sort of stupefaction, a dullness of the brain. She picked up a magazine, but soon dropped it on the floor, weary.

Still more startling, perhaps even slightly alarming, was the occurrence of delusions. She had come to Gorsedene expecting to find it nutty and slightly ridiculous. And so it was. But as the hunger took charge, she began to feel the atmosphere of the place to be menacing rather than comic. Quite ordinary happenings seemed somehow sinister. Was this, she wondered, the way people felt as they started to go mad?

She could not rid herself of the conviction, for instance, that Pelham Dimpsey and his wife were under such severe strain that they could scarcely conceal it. Just as the idea had come to her, early that morning, that Janet Dimpsey had been weeping, so now, as Pelham walked through the lounges, speaking to this patient or to that, he seemed to Kate to be struggling to suppress strong emotion.

She shook her head and told herself to stop imagining such nonsense. Probably the husband and wife had had a row over the housekeeping, or some such triviality. Even more probably they were not under strain at all, except in Kate's hunger-stoked fancy.

Similarly, when she went for a walk along the river bank in the early afternoon, she heard men's voices raised in what she was sure was angry argument. Round a bend in the towpath came Michael Neal and Philip Antrobus, side by side. There was nothing surprising in that. The journalist had taken the opportunity to talk with the man who, of all the patients at Gorsedene at that time, was most likely to provide copy for his column—the dispute in Washington over the defence contract. And Antrobus had not risked brushing off so influential a Washingtonian.

As they rounded the bend, Michael had one arm raised in a gesture. It seemed to Kate that, when he saw her, he dropped his arm in embarrassment.

That too, of course, was nonsense—a hunger distortion. Already Michael was smiling at her, quite calm, not in the least angry or disturbed, calling a greeting; and Antrobus stiffly nodding, acknowledging acquaintance.

If she went on like this, Kate murmured to herself as she walked by, she would simply have to eat something. The mere idea was enticing. She spent several minutes trying to decide whether she would start with something sweet or something savoury. Eventually, she came down for the savoury—soft roes on toast, for instance. Or angels on horseback.

According to the map in the entrance hall, she should soon come to another footbridge, which she intended to cross, and to return along the other bank to the footbridge in front of the Gorsedene lawn. But the bend in the river ended and she had a long view along a straight reach, with no footbridge. She must have misjudged the distance. As she was already starting to flag, she thought she had better circle back through the woods on her right. So she took the first footpath.

The woods were charming. They had been planted with such skill and taste that the green shades were varied from glade to glade, lit by the gentle glow of filtered sunlight, with here and there the first hints of autumn colours in preparation.

There was a sudden movement among the trees on her right. Kate shied nervously, for a moment terrified. Then she laughed crossly at herself. It was a squirrel, disturbed in the undergrowth, racing up a tree, peering round at her.

No woods are quite silent. Always there are rustlings, unexplained sighs, the creaking of branches even on windless days. And now she imagined she could hear voices, growing in strength as she walked, but uttering gibberish.

As she turned into the next glade she came upon three Indians. Startled, she halted. Then she saw that one, seated on a log and facing her, was Charan Lal, the Gorsedene porter. Another man was seated on a log with his back to her, and on the ground lounged a girl. Not gibberish, of course, but their own language, whichever of the multitude of Indian tongues that might be.

Lal gravely lowered his head towards her and said, "Good afternoon, madam."

The two others turned to face her, staring, saying nothing. The girl was exquisite.

Kate managed to reply with a "Good afternoon, Charan," and walked on.

Now what, she demanded angrily of herself, was sinister in that? Why should not the porter, with a couple of hours off duty, go to meet two of his friends? They were probably students like himself, working through the vacation in a nearby pub or café. To feel her encounter with them as menacing, terrifying, was simply irrational, another delusion.

Soft roes, she murmured to herself, on very thick toast, still doughy in the middle; or even fish soup with plenty of well-fried *croûtons*.

All she got, when she at last regained the terrace, was a cup of tea with lemon, which was being served by a boy she had seen working in the kitchen garden. Monday afternoon must be Lal's time off.

The Neals were not there. Phoebe Sadler was at a table at the far end of the terrace, but she had a man with her. So Kate was quite pleased when Bella, the pop singer, joined her, uninvited, and plunged at once into gossip and chatter. The two girls coming up the drive on horseback, and heading towards the riding stables at the rear, were the daughters of Lord Somebody-or-other, and Bella could tell a pretty story of how the younger, at a Mayfair club at which Bella was engaged to sing, was carrying on with a fellow who ran a strip-tease cellar in Soho. Had Kate seen the wog armed with a scimitar who stood guard outside the suite on the top floor where an Arab sheikh stayed hidden most of the time? He was getting through three bottles of scotch a day. Bella had this direct from the man in the kitchens who collected the cases as they arrived from the wine merchant. The guard was said to be a eunuch, but on no trustworthy evidence.

"Thought of having a go at him meself," she said, grinning, "just to find out. But he don't talk English."

Kate asked whether Bella knew the Dimpseys well. "They seem to be under a strain."

"Have you noticed that, too?" asked Bella. "It's only today. Usually they're all lovey-dovey, but this morning they were snapping at each other in the front room of their cottage. I was just passing, and the window was open. All of a sudden she sees me, so I waved and went on, not wanting to cause any embarrassment, like. They're the nicest folk. He is, anyway. And she's all right, too, though she does have a bit of a reputation with the men. I don't know what's up."

The patients on the terrace were turning their heads upwards, shading their eyes from the sun. There was a mutter in the sky, then a whirr. The helicopter was returning.

"That'll be Philip's," said Bella.

"Antrobus? You know him?"

The question seemed for a moment to disconcert Bella, as though she had been taken off guard.

"I met him," she then said. "One of the outfits in his group makes discs, and they were a dud lot, doing the wrong stuff and losing a lot of Philip's dough. So I was asked to come in and help. So I made some discs for them, and got some of my mates to come in, too. Philip's lot made a pile. I didn't have much to do with Philip himself. Business arrangement it was. But all of a sudden Philip comes along and asks me out to dinner."

She had completely regained her calm; perhaps it was only fancy that she had been momentarily jolted.

Bella winked at her: "If he ever asks you to dinner, luv, don't go."

The helicopter was touching down on the pad, jerking to a halt, the engine cutting, the shape of the rotors emerging as they slowed. First to get out was the thin man in the dark suit who had accompanied Antrobus the previous afternoon. He was carrying several document wallets. He was followed by the pilot, who this time secured the door of his helicopter before going into the house.

"Fellow in the dark pants is John Sherwood," Bella volunteered.

"Antrobus's secretary?"

"Bit more than that. He's Philip's man of business whose job it is to handle the dirty jobs—and there's plenty of 'em. I met him over that disc business. He was the chap who hired me." She grinned. "Not that there was anything dirty about that, let me tell you. Not him—not for Bella. But what I did find out later was that he come from Wolverhampton. Used to work in a factory, and carried out some sort of trick for Philip in the old days, when he was doing takeovers, fair or foul, usually foul. I had a boy-friend in Wolverhampton once, and Reg knew this Sherwood slightly. The bloody end, he was, Reg said. The limit in bastards, Reg called him."

She was silent for a while, then she said, "Reg and me was going to get spliced. We was even saving up for the deposit on the mortgage. That was before all this fame business started. Reg tried to take it, but he couldn't. He said that after a time he couldn't stand the jokes his mates were always dishing out at the works. Tools, they made. Good-class ironmongery. So Reg buggered off."

"Couldn't stand playing second fiddle to somebody who'd become a star?" asked Kate.

Bella sighed. "It weren't that. It was all the stories put around about me going to bed with all the boys in the band, and all that. It was just publicity. Reg knew that. But his mates didn't. I couldn't stop the publicity. I had these contracts, you see, luv, with clauses about publicity I'd not bothered to read, and anyway me agent said it was the usual thing."

She sighed again. "All the boys in the band!" she said contemptuously. "Me and Reg getting down to it on the couch in his front room, Saturday nights, when his Mum had gone to the bingo. That was what I wanted. He said we'd wed if I'd give up singing. Well, how could I? I'd got these bleeding contracts."

Kate was careful not to smile.

Over at the other end of the terrace she saw the Neals arriving, carrying tennis rackets.

"Be seeing you," she promised Bella, and went to meet them.

"You've had tea already?" asked Michael. "Glutton! I've a good mind to shame you by going without—doing a little bonus slimming."

"It wouldn't come amiss," said Mary.

"Did you get anything useful for your column from Philip Antrobus?" Kate asked.

"Not much," he said. "Did you enjoy your river walk? Get as far as the footbridge?"

"No. I came back through the woods."

Had his voice sounded constrained? Why had he so swiftly changed the subject? As she looked at Mary Neal, was it only Kate's fancy that there was a glance of desperation in her eyes?

Oh heavens, these hallucinations! Was Joan of Arc on a strict diet back there in Domrémy?

CHAPTER 4

THE EVENING was even warmer than of late. After the grapefruit, Kate wandered out towards the river. Crossing the lawn, she saw that the pilot of the helicopter was revisiting his machine. As she neared, he came down with a valise in his hand.

"Hallo," she said chattily. "You've been the biggest attraction of this place for two days." She was looking up into the helicopter cabin. "I've never been up in one of these things. It looks wonderful, floating about in the sky like that. Is it?"

"Not bad."

By the way he grunted it, he seemed a sullen young man. Yet he looked civil enough; attractive, really, in an overgrown schoolboy manner.

"May I get up and look inside?" she asked.

"Help yourself. I'm through with the damned thing."

"Has it gone wrong?"

"The machine's all right. It's the owner."

Kate felt curious. "No affair of mine, of course, but has he fired you?"

"He has not." The young man was angry. "I'm quitting. He'll find out."

"Doesn't he know? Haven't you told him?"

"I went to his room to tell him. He said to buzz off. He was busy with Sherwood. The crisis, of course."

"Crisis?"

"Seen the evening papers?"

"No. I'm taking a vacation from newspapers. I work for one. I write for the *Post*. Ever see it?

"Sometimes."

"My name's Kate Theobald. I quite often get a by-line."

"Then I suppose I must have seen your name some time."

"Constant reader," she murmured. "What crisis is this?"

"Been a big drop this afternoon in Antrobus shares on the Stock Exchange."

"So. It's a holding company, isn't it? A conglomerate. Antrobus Enterprises?"

He nodded. "The pound shares opened at four pounds fifty this morning. They closed tonight at three pounds ninety."

"Why?"

He shrugged. "Don't ask me. Ask John Sherwood."

"Is this why you're quitting? Antrobus conned you into buying his shares, and they've dropped more than you can afford?"

"Nothing like that. Personal reasons."

"Oh, then I won't ask."

She saw that Charan Lal, evidently now back on duty, was crossing the lawn towards them.

"Mr. Charles Pugh?"

"That's me."

"Mr. Antrobus asked me to give you a message, sir. He'll be free in ten minutes' time, and you're to go to his room."

The pilot flushed. "I take it he didn't say please."

Lal permitted himself a faint smile. "I don't really recall, sir."

Charles Pugh handed him the valise. "Okay. But will you please get me a taxi for the station in half an hour's time? And hang on to my grip until I come down?"

He strode away towards the house. The Indian was standing still, the valise in his hand, watching him go with apparently considerable interest.

"They've had a row," said Kate. "Mr. Antrobus is to be invited to fly his own helicopter home."

"Really, madam?" answered Lal, politely indifferent.

He started to walk towards the front door.

Suitably snubbed, Kate continued her walk across the lawn towards the river. But by now the sun was low in the sky, an evening breeze had got up, and the air above the towpath was alive with gnats. So she turned back and decided to go to her room, watch the telly, go to sleep early and forget the pangs of hunger. Though she had to admit that they were not as severe as they had been. Her stomach must be adapting. Wonderful thing, Nature.

She watched the programmes for a while, but then switched off and sat by the open window of her room. There was a moon, so she dowsed the light, lest it attract insects.

There was somebody on the small balcony of the room next to hers. When he spoke, she realized it was Philip Antrobus. She could not see the balcony but was sure of his voice.

"No," he said. "It's not on. Nothing like that."

A woman's voice answered from inside the room. It was too muffled, too distant for Kate to be able to make out the words; only the voice, and to be sure it was a woman's.

"The answer is no," said Antrobus. "This isn't something I'm going to buy."

His voice was fading, so he must be moving back into the room. There was a thin red flicker of a cigarette butt which he pitched into the quadrangle below. Then she could get only a mutter of voices. At one point she thought they were angry, but she could not hear distinctly enough to be sure.

Well, it was no business of hers. She looked at the travelling clock on the table by her bed. Good heavens, it was only eight o'clock. The rest of the evening stretched intolerably ahead. The best way of passing it was to sleep. So she undressed and got into bed. She started to read a magazine, but soon let it drop, and dozed off.

2

She could not at first place the sound that disturbed her. But as she gradually roused, she realized it was somebody laughing! she was not sure where. What did it matter, anyhow? She looked at the glowing dial of her travelling clock. It showed only twenty-five minutes to nine. Kate muttered irritably, turned on her side and dozed again.

She was half asleep when another noise roused her for the second time. She heard it only vaguely, still drowsy—

a sort of tapping noise. By the time she was fully awake it had ceased.

She glanced at the clock. Only five minutes past nine. Usually she was such a sound sleeper. Vague noises would not wake her. It must be this damned starvation diet that had jagged her nerves.

Now there was no particular noise; but then a thud, as though somebody had dropped something heavy. She listened, recalling wryly the joke about the hotel guest waiting in an agony of nerves all night for the man in the next room to throw down his second boot. There was no second boot, no repetition of the thud. She lay back on the pillow, closed her eyes, and after a few minutes dropped into sleep once more.

Next time she woke it was not because of a noise. Everything was silent. It was simply the pangs of hunger, now recurring strongly, like the gripes. She felt not only hungry, but miserable and desperately lonely. She wished like hell that Henry were there beside her, just to be able to talk to him. At the idea she reached for the telephone by her bed. She would talk to him, if only, as she hoped, he had got home by now. The clock. Ten minutes to ten o'clock.

There was no response. She shook the phone irritably, then pressed the lever up and down. According to the Gorsedene brochure the switchboard stayed open until eleven o'clock every night. She waited. Still no response.

Is this what she would be paying £100 a week for, if she were actually paying? she demanded of the night.

She put the phone down. But she still longed to talk to Henry. Vaguely she recalled that there was a public phone booth somewhere in the place, but she could not remember where she had seen it. Probably in the entrance hall. Should she summon the energy to go down? She hesitated, but then decided that she would. Putting on her dressing-gown, she opened her room door.

A man in pyjamas and dressing-gown was passing along the corridor.

"Oh, I say," she asked, "do you happen to know where the coinbox phone is? I can't get a reply from the switchboard."

"I've no idea."

He walked quickly on.

No need to be damned rude about it, Kate thought, and almost said. But then she realized who he was, John Sherwood, Antrobus's man of business. According to Bella's ex-boy-friend in Wolverhampton, damned rudeness was what you'd expect from John Sherwood anyway. Particularly as he seemed wrought up and angry. He had probably just been to see his boss in the room next door and been slanged about the Stock Exchange business.

She looked along the corridor, now empty. Oh hell, it was a long way to the entrance hall. She returned to bed. But she had been so thoroughly woken that she could not get off to sleep again.

She switched on her bedside lamp and reached for the magazine she had dropped. She tried to read, but soon found that she simply was not taking in the words, let alone the meaning.

With a sigh she dropped the magazine and looked at her clock. It was only a quarter past ten.

She still longed to talk to Henry, so she reached for the phone. But although she waited for several minutes, and kept on twitching the receiver rest, there was still no response. Whoever was supposed to be manning the switchboard obviously was not there.

So she took some coins from her handbag, put them in her gown pocket, and went out again to look for the public booth.

The corridor was no longer empty. A woman was standing in the open doorway of Philip Antrobus's room, arguing with a man who was trying to push past her to go in.

"Don't be silly," the man was saying. "I have to have it. There are reasons."

It was Michael Neal, she saw with surprise. The woman was his wife, Mary.

At that moment Mary saw her and clutched her husband's arm. She looked terrified.

Michael turned and saw Kate. She thought that for a moment he was startled, too, but practically at once he was smiling at her.

"Well, hallo," he said. "I do hope we haven't disturbed you."

"Oh, no."

"Philip Antrobus phoned our room ten minutes ago and asked us to come along for a nightcap."

"But he isn't here," cut in Mary quickly.

"Odd behaviour," said Michael, smiling again. "I suppose millionaires are privileged. They have a special sort of incivility. Which won't stop me telling him what I think of him tomorrow morning. Well, good night, Kate. Come on, darling. We're not waiting around for him."

He took her arm and they went off along the corridor.

Kate looked after them, slightly puzzled. She had not been able to get an answer from the switchboard ten minutes ago. Perhaps it was only that the line to her room was faulty.

The Neals had left the door ajar to Antrobus's room. Without quite knowing why she felt curiosity, Kate edged it wider and looked in.

The bedside lamp was alight. It was a larger room than hers, and more luxurious. A glass door opened on to the little balcony. That, too, was ajar. She went across to the balcony. It was an added asset. Philip Antrobus must have been sunbathing there during the afternoon; the parasol was still cocked over the long wicker chair, and the book he had been reading was still open on the table beside it.

She turned back into the room. How much extra, she wondered, did he pay for it?

The door to the toilet was ajar. Did a millionaire have to put up with a shower, like the common herd of patients, she wondered, walking towards it, amused, or did he get a proper bath with gold taps?

She pushed open the door, gasped, bit her knuckle.

He was hanging by the cord of his dressing-gown, which was tied to a water pipe close to the ceiling. The stool on which he must have been standing lay on its side against the wall, where he must have kicked it once he had the cord round his neck.

His tongue protruded, swollen, from his mouth. His eyes were staring. There was a limpness about the arms and the pyjama-clad legs dangling inside the silken dressing-gown with the Chinese dragon worked on it, that was somehow even more terrifying than the distorted face.

3

She stumbled back towards the bed, reaching for the telephone. Perhaps this one would work. As it did. After a short pause, a response.

"Can you put me through to Mr. Dimpsey?"

"This is Pelham Dimpsey speaking."

"Mr. Dimpsey, this is Kate Theobald. I'm in Mr. Antrobus's room." She heard the little gasp of astonishment. "Please come quickly. Something awful has happened."

"Awful?"

"Philip Antrobus has hanged himself."

She heard the phone smack down at the other end, abruptly, as though he had dropped it. She put hers down, sat on the edge of the bed and waited. It was then she became aware of the odour of whisky. She looked around. A bottle three parts empty, stood with a syphon and glasses on a side table. Philip Antrobus should not have been drinking alcohol, she murmured wryly to herself, the rules of the establishment were quite firm about that.

Dimpsey was there in a minute, breathing fast after running upstairs.

Kate pointed to the door of the bathroom, not looking. He hurried in, gasped with horror—almost a shout—then came hastily out, searching.

Understanding, Kate handed him a table knife from a plate of oranges by the bedside. He went back into the bathroom. She had to follow. He could not have managed it alone.

Indeed, he was standing there, knife in hand, badly shaken, helpless.

Kate took the knife. "I'll cut the cord above his head. You take his weight."

She righted the overturned stool and climbed up on it, shuddering as one of the limp arms brushed against her. Dimpsey, obeying like an automaton, encircled the legs with one of his arms, the back of the body with the other.

Kate cut as fast as she could. The knife was not very sharp.

"I'm nearly through," she warned. "Be ready."

As Antrobus's body fell, Dimpsey staggered badly under the weight. She thought he would collapse. But he managed to right himself and carry the dead man into the bedroom, letting him drop on to the bed.

Then he grabbed the phone and got a response.

"Get me through to Dr. Williams quickly!" He held on with one hand, tugging nervously with the other at a strand of his hair. "Hallo. Is that you, Ralph? Pelham here. Please come round as fast as you can. There's been a fatality. One of the patients has hanged himself . . . What's that? I don't think there's a hope, but maybe you, as a doctor . . . Anyway, please come fast. Come to the main entrance. I'll have somebody there to meet you."

He hung up, then spoke again. "Lal, Dr. Williams will arrive in a few minutes. Bring him straight to Mr. Antrobus's room. And quietly. Don't let anybody notice."

He put down the phone and looked at Kate, helpless.

"The police," she said.

"Police? Do we have to?"

"Of course you have to."

"But the awful publicity . . ."

Kate reached across for the phone. "Mr. Dimpsey wants to speak to the local police station."

She waited until she heard the connection, then handed the phone to Dimpsey.

"Is that Sergeant Grey? Sergeant, I have a fatality to report, I'm sorry to say. One of the patients has hanged himself . . . In his bathroom, with the cord of his dressing-gown. I thought I ought to report it at once . . . Yes, of course come round, if you think it necessary. Come to the main entrance. Can you come in plain clothes? Oh, good. I want as little fuss as possible, you understand, because of the other patients."

When the policeman had rung off, Dimpsey phoned the porter to show the sergeant up when he arrived, but very discreetly, for heaven's sake. Then he dropped into a chair by the window, as far from the bed as he could get, and sank his head in his hands, moaning.

Kate wandered round the room. Antrobus's clothes were all neatly put away. On one table near the wall his business wallets stood alongside files of documents, carefully stacked. Only one item was askew, at the front of the table; a typescript of a book. She glanced at the title—*The Vice Kings*. She had never heard of the author, Heinz Karasak.

It seemed improbable reading for a city tycoon. Idly she turned the pages. Slipped among them was a set of photostats of articles, also by Heinz Karasak, obviously from a cheap pulp magazine and, by the spelling, American.

The first article was illustrated by a photograph of a man and woman, all dolled up, walking from a huge car towards the entrance to a restaurant.

Kate started at the picture, startled. She looked quickly round at Pelham Dimpsey. He was still slumped in the chair, head in hands.

On impulse, she lifted the typescript and thrust it inside her dressing-gown.

"I'm going to my room next door to get a handkerchief," she told him. "I'll come straight back."

He looked up and nodded.

In her own room she pushed the typescript among her underclothes in a drawer.

4

As she returned to Antrobus's room, Lal was showing in the doctor and the policeman, who had evidently arrived simultaneously. When he had delivered them, the porter went back down the stairs.

The doctor was elderly, white-haired, but brisk, competent. He went straight to the bed, felt the body, glanced at the livid mark round the throat where the cord had bitten and at the bruising starting to show around it, then straightened.

"He has been dead for at least an hour, probably longer. There's no question of resuscitation."

Sergeant Grey, a thickset, plodding man—Kate knew the type so well, very worthy, not very bright—asked where the body had been found. Dimpsey led him into the bathroom. After a few minutes the sergeant returned and went to Kate.

"Mr. Dimpsey tells me you found the deceased, madam."

"That's right. You want a statement?"

"If you please," he said, already getting out his notebook and ballpoint. If only it had been a pencil, she thought, he could have given it the traditional lick.

She gave him her name and Chelsea address. "I'm a patient here, Sergeant, and I happen to have the room next door. At a quarter past ten o'clock I wanted to phone my husband at home. I know the time because I looked at my travelling clock. But I couldn't get a reply from the Gorsedene switchboard. So a little later, I suppose five minutes or so later, I left my room to go downstairs to find a coinbox phone booth."

"There are two booths in the entrance hall," volunteered Pelham Dimpsey. "I don't know why Mrs. Theobald could not get the switchboard. Lal, the porter, mans it after nine-thirty. He must have been called away on some errand. Patients often ring for service."

"As I passed this room," continued Kate, "I saw that the door was open. I thought I heard a noise inside—I must have imagined it. So I looked in. The bathroom door was open, and I saw the man hanging there. I phoned downstairs quickly and Mr. Dimpsey answered."

"I happened to be crossing the hall, and saw the switchboard was unmanned," said Dimpsey.

"And that's all, madam?"

"That's all, Sergeant. Except that I righted the stool to help Mr. Dimpsey cut the body down. When I first looked in, the stool had been kicked over on its side against the far wall."

There seemed, she thought, no point in involving the Neals—at any rate, not until she had sorted out a couple of points with them.

"I'll get a formal statement typed out, Mrs. Theobald. If you would please come to the station tomorrow to sign it . . ."

"Of course, Sergeant."

The doctor had returned to Antrobus's body. The sergeant was engaged in questioning Pelham Dimpsey.

So Kate quietly left the room. There was something pressing to do.

She went quickly downstairs. There was nobody in the entrance hall. After a brief search, she found the phone booths round the corner from the reception desk. She dialled the *Daily Post*, asked urgently for a telephone reporter, and put over the story—simply, briefly, no details. She was switched to the news desk.

"Hang on a minute, Kate," said the night news-editor. "I've got Butch on the line—rang him at home. I'm going to link him through to you."

Then there was Butch. "Kate, are you absolutely sure of this story?"

"Of course I am."

"Antrobus Enterprises took a bad beating on the Stock Exchange this afternoon. When we give the news of his suicide, they'll fall through the floor. Millions of pounds will be lost. If there's even the slightest, wildest chance of a mistake, for everybody's sake tell me. If you are wrong, it could break the paper."

"I know it's Philip Antrobus. I've seen him here for a couple of days, and spoken with him. Some time back, I knew him because I interviewed him. I know he's hanged, because I was the one who found him, hanging by his dressing-gown cord from a pipe near the ceiling of his bathroom."

"His private bathroom? How come?"

"It's an involved story, Butch. I can't tell you over the phone. Trust me. It's okay."

When he had gone, she dialled her own flat. Henry answered, sleepily. "What's wrong?"

"I found a patient here, in the next room to mine, hanged from a pipe in his bathroom. Never mind how I found him. I'll tell you when we meet. It's Philip Antrobus."

She heard Henry's low whistle. "That could break the whole market. It's touchy enough already. Did you know there was a slump in Antrobus's shares this afternoon? Oh, you did. When it's known that he has hanged himself immediately after . . . Well, I don't know how far it might go."

"Henry," she said, "I want you to come here, tomorrow morning, please darling."

"But why? What on earth can I do to help?"

"Hold my hand, darling. I'm uneasy. Something's not right, though I'm not sure what it is."

"A man hanging himself isn't right. But why should that make you uneasy? It's finished with. Oh, some fuss with the police, of course. If you will go prying into strange men's bathrooms . . ."

"Henry, I'm not in the mood for seeing the funny side. There's something very odd. I can't tell you on the phone. It may have absolutely no significance, but it did suggest to me a very pertinent question."

"Which is?"

"If you were going to hang yourself, would you go on a health cure first?"

There was silence at the other end. Then he said, "I'll drive down tomorrow morning."

"Don't get here before half past eleven, darling. I've got my treatments until then."

CHAPTER 5

THE CHATTER in the steam bath-house next morning could be, of course, of nothing else. All the heads protruding from the cabinets were nodding vigorously in discussion as to why he did it, and surely there was a woman behind it all, and how much money had he left, and how about the wife he'd just divorced, would she get the dough, or had he cut her off out of spite?

When Phyllis had settled Kate into her steam bath—the same place as yesterday, with Bella's topknot as neighbour—the heads swivelled towards her, wanting to know, not why he had done it, but how gruesome the body had looked, hanging there. "All naked, wasn't he?" asked one.

"Oh no. He was wearing his pyjamas and that Chinese silk dressing-gown with the dragon on it. Quite proper and decent, I assure you."

"Except the bastard was dead," said Bella.

"Except that he was dead," Kate granted.

"If it'd been me," declared a somewhat elderly head with strongly-dyed red hair, further round the room, "I'd have fainted clean away."

"Not her," Bella confided to Kate beneath the chatter. "I'll tell you about her later. Three husbands she's had, all old and rich, and all soon dead, so that's three corpses she's come across that didn't give her a turn."

From the far side one of the heads demanded loudly, "How did you come to find him?"

"I'm in the next-door room," Kate told her. She related how she had gone to look for a phone, seen Antrobus's door open, thought she heard a noise and looked in.

There was something of a hush for a long minute. Then the hubbub of chatter broke out again.

"There's not one of them believes you," murmured Bella, grinning.

"Do you?" asked Kate.

"Course I do, luv. You're not his sort."

"What sort would you say is his?"

"Not me," said Bella, laughing. "One dinner-party— that's all I ever got to. I left in a hurry, by boat. On his motor cruiser it was, up the Thames near Maidenhead. Quite a do! I'll tell you about it sometime."

"I'd love to hear."

"But not down here with all these big ears about."

The steam was comfortably relaxing. Almost, Kate felt, she could doze off.

"I'd forgotten he'd just divorced his wife," she said lazily. "Some row about the child, too, wasn't there?"

"Over custody," Bella told her. "A little girl they had, must be three or four years old now."

"Did the custody case ever get into court?" asked Kate, trying to recall the story. "I don't remember it."

"Hasn't come up yet, seemingly," said Bella.

"Wasn't she an actress or something!"

"Used to be a model, the usual thing. Come of some posh family, but flat broke. Also the usual thing. She's a complete bitch. Why did he marry her? Maybe Daddy had a shotgun. And getting spliced didn't make no difference to Philip. I've seen him with lots of other women. There's a club I sing at, one of the smart places, Mayfair. He's often there with some woman or other. But never his missus." She smiled mischievously. "Want to know who was one of the last women I see him with, couple of times? The boss's wife, here."

"You mean here at Gorsedene? Janet Dimpsey?" asked Kate, surprised.

" 'Sright."

"You mean, she and Philip Antrobus . . . ?"

"I don't mean anything, luv. How would I know? I expect he was just taking her out to supper because her old man had gone off his lettuce. Here, Phyllis, luv, I'm cooked. Get me out, there's a dear."

When she was extracted and wrapped in her towel, she winked at Kate. "See you after massage."

Norah, the masseuse, seemed depressed. When she had Kate on the table in the cubicle, face down, she pounded her spine in silence.

"Am I improving?" Kate asked after a while.

Norah grunted. "Yes, a little."

Again silence. Kate began to feel awkward. "Dreadful thing," she said chattily, "Mr. Antrobus."

"Got us all upset," Norah agreed. "The staff, I mean."

"He'd been here before, hadn't he?"

"Yes, often."

Remembering Bella's hint, Kate asked, "Did he know Mr. and Mrs. Dimpsey well, then?"

"Of course. They're old friends. That's why Mr. Dimpsey got the place."

"Got the place? I don't quite understand."

"Gorsedene belongs to Mr. Antrobus—or I suppose I ought to say, did belong to him."

"He owned Gorsedene?"

"One of his companies. It was all very complicated, I believe, because of tax or something. That's what I've heard, anyhow. But, of course, Mr. Antrobus controlled the company, so he was the actual owner. He bought it about five years ago. Before that it was owned by some property millionaire. When Mr. Antrobus bought it, he put Mr. Dimpsey in to run it. But it wasn't just the old pals' act. Mr. Dimpsey already had a great reputation as a nature therapist, and he has made a wonderful place of Gorsedene, best known in the world, I'd say. He's a very clever man, Mr. Dimpsey."

"Mrs. Dimpsey seems very nice, too," said Kate.

Norah said nothing.

"If it's owned by a company," Kate went on, "I suppose that Philip Antrobus's death won't make any difference."

"That's what's worrying us all," Norah admitted. "Gorsedene doesn't make much profit, you know."

"Not much profit, at those charges?"

"Costs are terribly high, Mrs. Theobald. Patients never really believe this. But I assure you it's so. All this equipment costs the earth—and maintaining it is expensive, too. Then it has to be changed quite often. Gorsedene has to have the very latest. That's what its reputation rests on. If you come here, you pay a lot, but you get the finest treatment in the world, and good service, too."

Kate nodded. "First rate. So I suppose staff costs must be high, stuck out in this remote country."

"There've been rumours lately that it's actually running at a loss," said Norah. "Mr. Antrobus wouldn't have minded. He had so many companies. But now . . . If they put it on the market, it might not sell. Even if it did, what we fear is that any other owner wouldn't keep up Gorsedene standards. There'd be redundancies, cutting back. It would be an awful shame if that happened to Gorsedene. Most of us would think of leaving anyhow, even if we weren't fired. There now, I think that will be enough for today. You may find your back a little stiff for an hour or so. But then it'll ease off. It's tomorrow you're trying the underwater massage, isn't it? Well, don't let Mavis keep you in it too long. Not the first time."

"Thanks," said Kate. "I'll remember that. And I shouldn't worry too much about the future. A place as good as Gorsedene won't be let go."

2

Her back was slightly stiff. So she changed into a swimsuit and got into the pool, swimming gently, then floating idly. The sun was warm, except when a small cloud drifted across it, but was soon past.

When she left the pool she thought it wiser to change from her wet swimsuit, so she went up to her room for a cotton dress.

The phone rang. "Mr. Theobald is here, madam."

"Send him up, please."

When he arrived she kissed him eagerly. "Am I glad to see you!"

Henry smiled. "Starvation getting you down?"

"Curiously enough, not. It's a very old sensation. At first it's absolute hell. But now, after a couple of days, I scarcely remember most of the time that I'm eating practically nothing. And I think I'm even starting to feel a tiny bit healthier. But that's not it."

"Antrobus, of course."

She nodded.

"You got away with it until the late editions," he told her.

"I haven't seen the papers. The others picked it up? That was inevitable. I expect Butch held it as long as he dared. They did me proud, eh, Henry? Was it the splash, and most of page one?"

"It could scarcely be less," he assured her. "It has knocked the City sideways. I picked up an early *Standard* on the way here. The jobbers marked everything down heavily directly the market opened—but not heavily enough. The FT index nose-dived. Antrobus Enterprises were almost unsaleable, of course. They were down to two pounds fifty by eleven this morning, and very few takers. There must be some fearful scandal, with the wraps just coming off. He must have known that. Hence the suicide."

"If it was," said Kate.

Henry took the chair by her table and motioned her to sit on the bed.

"Now then, Kate, no more mystery. What is it?"

"As I told you on the phone, what puzzled me at first was why a man who intended to kill himself should start by taking a health cure."

"The explanation is simple. He was under strain, but thought he'd get through the crisis all right. So he came down here to unwind. But on Monday afternoon the bears started selling his shares short—in very large amounts, I assure you. Before I came this morning I rang up Peter Lane—he's an old college friend of mine who has a partnership in a broker's office. It was a massive bear raid."

"Would you please explain to a simple little woman exactly what a bear raid is?"

"It's selling shares you haven't got, in the hope of being able to buy them at a lower price before settling day arrives, and you have to pay for them. Suppose you sold one thousand shares, which you hadn't got, at one pound each. Your account with your broker would be one thousand pounds in credit. Then the price drops to 50p. So you buy one thousand shares at 50p, and your account with your broker is debited five hundred pounds. On settling day you collect the difference—five hundred pounds in cash, less commission and stamp charges. Get it?"

"I think so," she said doubtfully.

"Bears usually operate when the whole market is falling. But if an operator knew, through leaked information, that a particular company was in trouble, he could make a bear raid on its shares—sell them although he had none—and wait for the price to drop to take his profit. That happened to Antrobus Enterprises shares yesterday on a big scale. When Antrobus heard of that, he knew that the secret, whatever it was, had leaked. Did any of his people come down here that afternoon or evening?"

"Yes. His man of business. A man named John Sherwood. He came in the Antrobus helicopter. It's an impressive arrival, Henry."

"There you are then, Antrobus gets news of the Stock Exchange uproar—by phone from his office, obviously. He tells Sherwood to come and report. Sherwood, who was probably in the know about the hidden scandal, tells him it's all up. So Antrobus hangs himself."

"If that were all," said Kate. "Do you know who Michael Neal is?"

"The Washington journalist?"

"Yes. He's here with his wife, Mary."

She described to him how she had found them at the door of Antrobus's room, then out of curiosity gone in and discovered the man hanging, and had alerted the director, Pelham Dimpsey.

Kate went to the drawer of her dressing-table and pulled out the typescript and the photostats of articles. Henry took them, puzzled.

"*The Vice Kings*. What on earth has this muck to do with it?"

"Everything in Philip Antrobus's room was very neat and tidy. All his clothes were carefully put away. The soda syphon, glasses and bottle of whisky—of which he'd drunk about two-thirds, strictly against Gorsedene rules—

were symmetrically arranged on a silver tray. He had brought a lot of wallets and business papers with him, and Sherwood arrived with more. They were meticulously stacked on a large table by the wall. Only one thing was out of place—this typescript. It lay on the front edge of the table, almost sliding over on to the floor, as though it had been thrown down carelessly or hastily. It seemed odd to me. So when Dimpsey was plunged into deep gloom and wasn't noticing, I picked it up. *The Vice Kings.* Odd reading for a tycoon—but everyone to his own taste. Then those photostats slipped out from between the typed pages, and I saw that picture."

"Well?" asked Henry, staring at it.

"The man going into that restaurant in New York is one of the vice kings—indeed, the vice emperor. I've been reading the thing through during the night. It's not great prose, but meaty. The book, by the same author, is a lot meatier than the articles. He developed his theme when he wrote at length."

"I'm still at a loss," said Henry.

"The name of the man in the photo is Victor Zucconi."

"I've heard of him. The FBI or somebody got him in the end, didn't they?"

"According to our author, Heinz Karasak, he was arrested about five years ago. There was the usual long legal battle, but last year he lost it and went down for a minimum of twenty-five years. Author Karasak is confident, however, that his vice empire has survived him and is being run by some of his old associates. He doesn't name any of them in the articles, but he's bolder in the book and he indicts at least four. He says there are yet others profiting on the quiet—sleeping partners, as you might say, if that's not too appropriate. In the book he hints, though he doesn't actually state, that one of them is the girl in that picture, which was taken five years ago, just before Zucconi got pulled in, and charged."

"The girl," said Henry patiently.

"It's a badly printed picture, rather smudged, and the photostat makes it even foggier, of course. The girl is named as Mary Pastorelli. It's a five-year-old photo, so she will have changed somewhat. But I have an uneasy conviction that she's now Mary Neal."

Henry whistled softly.

After a pause, he said, "You are implying that somebody—presumably Philip Antrobus himself—was blackmailing the Neals and had to be silenced? Oh, come on, Kate. Why should a millionaire blackmail a journalist?

"He was saying to her, when I saw them outside Antrobus's door, "Don't be silly. I have to have it. There are reasons.""

Henry considered. "So then you go on to deduce that, as Antrobus had to be silenced, Michael Neal silenced him. But that becomes absurd, for several obvious reasons. The first is, Antrobus had been dead for at least an hour, and Neal hadn't got the typescript. The second is even more convincing. It's probably a physical impossibility. I admit that a man who is hanged hasn't necessarily hanged himself. But you are postulating that a fully-grown, active man is overcome and slung up to a pipe in his bathroom ceiling, without making a fight—which would leave traces, bound to—and without making enough noise for you to hear it next door."

"Drugged?" suggested Kate.

"That wouldn't do. It would be discovered at the autopsy. In those circumstances the coroner is sure to require one. Yes, there will be an inquest. But even if you assume the man could be overcome, I very much doubt if any man could then haul him up by his dressing-gown cord to a pipe near the ceiling. I'd like to have a look at that pipe . . . "

"No need," Kate told him. "My bathroom is smaller, but the same pipe runs across the ceiling. I think it must be part of the original plumbing—it's very stout—and it runs the length of the bathrooms."

Henry went into her bathroom and stared at the pipe.

While he was doing so, she looked at her watch. "Henry, there's one thing. I have to go to the local police station to sign my statement. Will you drive me?"

"Of course. Now I've seen the pipe, Kate, I'm sure it's impossible—or, at least, highly improbable. Besides, you're forgetting Antrobus's perfectly good motive for committing suicide—the sudden bear raid on his shares, which told him clearly that somebody knew something and the scandal was soon coming out."

"That's tenable," Kate agreed, "if it was suicide. But suppose there is no scandal. Suppose, when it's all investigated, Antrobus Enterprises turns out to be quite sound. Then there'd be no reason for Antrobus to hang himself."

"My dear girl, you really must stop imagining impossibilities. The selling of the shares started yesterday afternoon, while the man was alive and well, and taking a health cure. The only possible explanation of that is that the bears knew something was wrong with Antrobus Enterprises, so they were selling short. If nothing were wrong with the group, it would imply that the bears knew the shares would slump today, Tuesday, because they knew on Monday afternoon that Antrobus was going to kill himself on Monday evening."

"Or that somebody was going to kill him."

Henry shook his head sadly at her. "It's lack of food making you light-headed. I'll drive you to the police station to sign your formal statement. That might clear some of the nonsense from your imagination."

3

Sergeant Grey kept them waiting a while. However, Kate said not to mind. There is a charm about small-town police stations—a bareness, an occupation with the minutiae of law-and-order, small boys reporting lost bicycles, irritated motorists paying parking fines, frequent cups of milky tea, that sort of thing. Enjoy it.

When they were shown to an inner room, Sergeant Grey, seated at a wooden table, looked enquiringly at Henry.

"He's my husband, Sergeant. I'd rather like to have him with me. He's a lawyer."

Sergeant Grey assented doubtfully and invited Kate to be seated; there was no third chair for Henry. The policeman handed her a typed statement made from his notes of the previous night.

"If there's anything you want to add, Mrs. Theobald, or any changes you want to make . . . "

Reading it quickly, Kate shook her head.

"May I see?" asked Henry.

When he had read it, he handed it back to her without comment. She smiled sweetly at him, knowing what he was thinking. Then she signed the statement.

"Will you be here on Friday, ma'am?" enquired the sergeant.

"Unless I'm carried off by malnutrition."

Sergeant Grey paid no attention to the joke; perhaps he hadn't seen it.

"You'll be wanted as a witness at the inquest," he said. "The coroner's court is just behind here, in the next street. Friday morning, eleven o'clock."

"But that's my massage appointment," complained Kate.

Henry asked, "Has the coroner required an autopsy, Sergeant?"

"He has, sir. He's a fussy man, our coroner."

"You think an autopsy unnecessary?"

"Don't you, sir? By the time I got there, the deceased was laid out on the bed. Your wife and Mr. Dimpsey had cut him down. But they both saw him hanging in the bathroom. I can testify to the mark of the cord round his throat, and the condition of the mouth, tongue and eyes. But the coroner wants to be satisfied."

"I suppose," said Henry, "that an autopsy might show that he was drugged."

Sergeant Grey smiled slowly, solidly. "Not unless the drug was Scotch whisky, sir. The room was still smelling of it when I got there. Still, what the coroner says, goes. So an autopsy there must be. The remains have been removed to the hospital, sir. Dr. Williams'll do the post mortem this afternoon. There's already been identification by Mr. John Sherwood, who was the deceased's business consultant."

"Not by a member of the family?" asked Kate.

"Seemingly there's only an infant daughter, Mrs. Theobald. Mr. Sherwood says there are no other near relatives. There was a Mrs. Antrobus, but Mr. Sherwood tells me she and Mr. Antrobus were divorced. We've made some enquiries, but so far we can't find out where the lady is. Not that it matters much, seeing as she's not his wife any longer."

"Surely she must be found, to look after the child—unless she has custody already."

"That'll be a matter for the lawyers. Mr. Sherwood says, ma'am. The child is at the deceased's house in London. There's no need to worry, Mr. Sherwood says. She's being looked after by her nanny, as well as the housekeeper."

"That's a relief," said Kate, rising to go.

Driving back to Gorsedene, Henry asked her, "Why didn't you say anything in your statement about seeing Mr. and Mrs. Neal at the door to Antrobus's room?"

"Why should I, darling? You're all convinced it was suicide, so where's the relevance?"

Henry was frowning. "It was a bit stupid, Kate. You'll have to give evidence at the inquest on the same lines as your statement, and you'll be on oath. So you can scarcely repeat that you heard a noise in Antrobus's room, which was why you went in."

"But I did hear a noise in his room. Not precisely at that moment, but earlier in the evening. Several noises."

"What noises?"

"I'll have to try to remember. I'll sit down quietly and try to think back. There was a woman there early in the evening. I heard Antrobus talking to her. Then there was laughter at some stage, and there was an odd noise—tapping, slapping, something like that—and once there was a thud. I'll try to reconstruct my recollections and write them down. Henry, you are staying, aren't you?"

"Not at Gorsedene," he assured her, laughing. "But I'll stay. I've put my bag into the Crown in the town, and taken a room there for a few nights. I'll be around if you need me, though I don't see any reason why you should."

Kate was serious. "I can't get rid of my feeling that it wasn't suicide. I know you think I'm dreaming it up. But there's that typescript, and the Neals. And there are the noises. And there's something else that's wrong, I know there is, though I can't place it. I've seen something that was wrong, without really taking in what I saw, but just getting an uneasy impression of wrongness, if you know what I mean?"

He humoured her affably. "All right, Kate. You think it wasn't suicide. I'm sure it was. But I'll go along with you this far—it was suicide forced on the man by the collapse of his shares. And there was certainly some funny business there."

"How can we find out what it was?"

He considered. "Tell you what. I'll drop you off at Gorsedene, and drive back to London, to have a quiet word with Peter Lane. Who's he? I told you, darling. An old friend of mine who's on the Stock Exchange. Whatever the funny business was, he'll probably have an idea of it— uncanny the efficient way the grapevine works in the City."

"While you're away," she said, "I'll see what I can do with Michael Neal. I think I can approach him tactfully. I doubt whether I'd get much out of his wife. You'll be back tonight, won't you?"

"Sure. It isn't all that far, and I can do most of the journey on the motorway. I'll be back well in time for dinner at the Crown." He turned his head to grin at her. "I had a look at the table d'hôte menu for today. It's celery soup, roast beef and treacle tart."

"Beast!"

CHAPTER 6

KATE WALKED BACK along the driveway to Gorsedene. She had told Henry to drop her at the entrance gates, for she wanted exercise. "And you get off to London. If you hurry, you'll be in time for lunch at your club."

For a couple of hundred yards the driveway lay alongside the river bank. The river, overhung by willows and planted here and there with rushes, murmured quietly and gleamed in the midday sunshine. Then the driveway turned aside from the river, passed through a small wood, and emerged to a charming view of the director's cottage on the right, and the main Gorsedene buildings farther off.

Pelham Dimpsey was writing at a desk in the front window of his cottage. Looking up, he saw Kate and motioned to her with agitation. Then he hastened through the front door.

"Mrs. Theobald. I've been trying to locate you."

"My husband drove me to the police station to sign a formal statement."

"Oh, of course. This appalling business. I was there at eight o'clock this morning. Sergeant Grey insisted. Though there was nothing I could tell him that he hadn't seen for himself. Mrs. Theobald, may I detain you for a moment? Would you please come in?"

He led her into the room in which he had been writing; a pleasant room, pale green panelling, most of the walls occupied by white bookshelves untidily stacked with a multitude and variety of books and magazines, a couple of indifferent but brightly-coloured landscapes, several framed photographs of his wife and the boy.

"Mrs. Theobald," he said, as they sat facing each other, he at his desk, she in a deep armchair, "I have a particular request to make. Please do not write anything more about Gorsedene and what has happened here in your newspaper."

"I couldn't possibly give any such undertaking," she protested. "I doubt if there'll be anything more to report about Mr. Antrobus's death. Sergeant Grey told me that his body has been taken away for an autopsy. We shall have a local correspondent covering the inquest on Friday. But if any more news does happen here at Gorsedene, I shall certainly report it. I am a newspaper reporter, Mr. Dimpsey."

"You are also our guest."

She could see that he felt ashamed of himself as he said it.

"If you let me have a bill at the end of my stay, I'll be happy to pay it. I shall remain for the week—unless you ask me to leave."

He held out his hands towards her in a helpless gesture.

"Forgive me, Mrs. Theobald. I should not have said that. But the consequences of your article in the *Daily Post* this morning have been catastrophic for me, and may well be for my establishment." He leaned forward earnestly. "There are at this moment six newspaper reporters waiting in the entrance hall to waylay me. I cannot even enter my own premises unmolested."

Kate smiled gently at him. He was so evidently under strain.

"If I hadn't chanced to be here, and to get a story into the *Post* this morning, it would have been in the evenings today, and all the dailies tomorrow. You can't keep a thing like this quiet."

"But at Gorsedene of all places! It will do us irreparable damage."

"As for the reporters in the hall, take my advice. Invite them here to your house, now, straight away. Give them some sherry. Answer any questions they ask you. Then they'll go and you'll be troubled no more. If you don't they'll hang around for days."

He gestured despairingly again. "I can't face it. My nerves are in shreds."

"I'll stay with you," she offered, "and handle them. It won't be too dreadful."

"Would you?" he asked eagerly, but then doubtfully. "Must I? The easiest way, you tell me?"

Kate nodded. So Dimpsey reached for the phone on his desk and told Charan Lal to bring the reporters over to the cottage. "Yes, right away, Lal."

He sank back in his chair, exhausted.

"I must apologize for this display of panic," he said contritely. "But this dreadful happening has hit me hard. Philip was such an old friend, of both my wife and myself. Indeed, Janet knew him longer than I. It was she who originally introduced him to me. The shock has knocked her up badly. She has had to go to bed with one of her migraines—and I was so confident she had conquered them. She has been taking herbal treatment for more than a year."

"Somebody was telling me," said Kate, "that Mr. Antrobus owned Gorsedene."

"Through one of his companies, yes. It was he who appointed me as director. He has always been so good to us. In recent months there has been an idea that I might be able to purchase Gorsedene for myself or, if that proved impractical, to lease it in some way. Philip was looking into all that. Janet went to London several times to discuss possibilities with him. Janet has the business brain in our partnership. I am hopeless at such things. I thought it might be carried off—my dearest dream." He stared hopelessly out of the window. "Now, of course, there is no longer any prospect."

Through the window she could see Charan Lal entering the garden with the reporters. Five of them she knew. The sixth was probably a local man.

Pelham Dimpsey followed her gaze. He massaged his fingers together nervously. There were beads of sweat forming at his temples and upper lip.

"Don't worry," Kate reassured him. "I'll handle it. Just answer any questions they ask you. Where's the sherry?"

He jerked from his chair and crossed to a corner cupboard. He was fussing with the decanter and the glasses when Lal ushered the reporters in.

"Hallo," said Kate.

"Hallo, Kate," said one of them. "You have the devil's luck."

"Merit and conscientious hard work are sometimes rewarded with a small break," she told him, smiling. "Let me introduce Mr. Pelham Dimpsey, the director of Gorsedene. As you know from the *Post* this morning, he was with me when we took Philip Antrobus's body down."

She introduced him to the five she knew, giving him their names and newspaper.

"And of course I know Mr. Robinson," said Dimpsey to the sixth. He seemed to have recovered his nerve, and had dried his face with a handkerchief. "If any of you gentlement would care for a glass of sherry . . ."

They all would. He offered Kate a glass, but she declined. "I'm on the diet, remember?"

"Ah yes, of course." He hesitated for a moment, then poured himself one.

When the reporters were served and seated, the questions began. Had Mr. Dimpsey any idea that Mr. Antrobus was depressed, in the sort of mood for suicide? No, not at all. He had been at Gorsedene for two days—he was a frequent visitor there—and he had seemed perfectly normal, just as he always was.

He was the owner of Gorsedene, wasn't he? Yes. That is to say, he was the chairman of the company that owned the establishment, and Pelham Dimpsey believed he held a majority of the company's shares, through another company. All very complicated, but in effect Mr. Antrobus was the owner.

So what would happen to Gorsedene now?

Raising his hands in his customary gesture of desperation, Dimpsey admitted he had no idea. It was clear from the newspapers that Philip's business affairs were in some sort of trouble. Until those problems had been sorted out, who could tell?

One questioner changed the line. Mr. Dimpsey knew Philip Antrobus's divorced wife, didn't he?

"Yes. My wife and I were personal friends of Phoebe Antrobus, as well as of Philip himself, for a number of years."

"Do you know where she is?"

"Gentlemen, I'm sorry, but I cannot say anything at all about Philip's private life. No, please excuse me. I will not discuss anything of that kind."

"We simply want to ask her about their daughter," cut in another reporter.

Kate tutted to herself; tactless. Pelham Dimpsey had stiffened at the remark, and did not reply.

There were a few more questions about finding the body, about Gorsedene itself, about nothing very much at all.

"There's really little I can add to the account which Mrs. Theobald wrote in the *Daily Post* this morning," said Dimpsey at last. "I'd like to be more helpful, but I have no more to tell you."

"Mr. Dimpsey's right," said Kate. "There was just this horrible business of my finding Philip Antrobus hanged, and calling Mr. Dimpsey in to take charge. We got the body down on the bed, and Mr. Dimpsey phoned hastily for a doctor and the police. And that's honestly all there is."

"Ghastly for you, Kate," one of them murmured sympathetically.

"Ghastly indeed."

When they had gone, Pelham Dimpsey thanked her for her help in what had been, for him, a frightening ordeal.

"What will they write in their newspapers?" he asked nervously. "That is what worries me, Mrs. Theobald. Your account in the *Daily Post* this morning, though frankly I shuddered when I saw it, was at least factual and straightforward. But now . . . There's nothing new to report. I fear they will write in an exaggerated manner about Gorsedene itself, and the people who come here—famous people, rich people."

Kate had to admit the probability.

"But the people who come here, our patients, are precisely the sort of people who deprecate that sort of publicity about a place. We shall be pilloried as a luxurious establishment where a prominent man commited suicide, and whose death led to turmoil and to many wealthy people losing a great deal of money."

"But that is what happened, Mr. Dimpsey. The facts are what count, not newspaper reports of them."

Pelham Dimpsey leaned back, shaking his head slowly.

"My poor, poor Gorsedene," he murmured sorrowfully.

2

Henry drove first to Chelsea. If he were to stay for the rest of the week at the Crown he would need some more clean shirts.

From his flat he tried to phone Peter Lane's office in the City. Every time he dialled it, the number was engaged. He knew that the office had at least five lines. 'Struth, they must be busy.

For all Kate's jeer, he did not bother to go to his club for lunch. It was almost too late anyhow. He went to the nearest pub for a beer and a hunk of French bread and cheddar cheese. Delicious.

From the phone in the pub he tried twice more to get Peter's office. The lines were still busy. So he walked to Sloane Square, took a Circle train to Mansion House and walked through the City to Copthall Buildings.

Peter's office was in turmoil. A girl at the reception desk told him that Mr. Lane was on the floor of the Exchange and she doubted if she could get hold of him. But at that moment he came through on the phone with a list of bargains completed. When he had finished, Mr. Theobald could talk to him.

"Hallo, Peter. Any chance of meeting when the session's over?"

"Certainly not before, Henry. This place has gone mad. I can't stop to talk even on the phone. We could meet at the office at, say, about five. Meanwhile, if you want a view of Bedlam, come over here and try the public gallery."

The public gallery was crowded, but Henry managed to get a view. The floor was like a disturbed ants' nest, black-coated men rushing everywhere, hubbub, prices changing minute by minute. Henry watched it for a while, then went out to find a café where he could get a cup of tea.

At five o'clock he returned to Peter's office.

"I'm going to be working here until God knows when," Peter said. "But if it's important . . ."

"I think it might be."

"Let's go round the corner to my club. I could do with an hour's break."

There were not many in the club in Cornhill.

"All in their offices licking their wounds—or preparing to jump out of the window," said Peter. "Drink?"

"It's a bit early. Oh well, a beer. Thanks."

When they were settled, Henry began, "You saw the *Post* this morning, about Kate finding Antrobus?"

"Absolutely fascinating, old man. It's what started all this disaster off. Not your wife's report, of course, but Antrobus's suicide. I've never known anything like it. I almost daren't think about where the Index stands. I hear the Chancellor is already being questioned in the House. Fat lot of good that'll do. Nobody has yet calculated how much has been wiped off share values. Must run into hundreds of millions."

"Not all because of Antrobus, surely."

"That was the trigger. There has been uneasiness for some time, as you must know. The market was due for a shake-out. But nothing on this scale. What we all fear is a major slump. It has happened before, of course—a leading financier suddenly breaking, even bumping himself off, and then panic that starts a downward spiral. However, what is it you're after?"

"I can't really tell you much about it," said Henry. "Kate has an idea that there's something odd going on behind this Antrobus business. And, of course, as a newspaperwoman . . ."

"Certainly odd," Peter agreed, taking a long pull at his beer. "When the bear raid started on Antrobus Enterprises yesterday afternoon, there were such ugly rumours flying round that there was already talk of a Stock Exchange enquiry. Suspected leak, of course. Nobody has had time today to think any more about that. But it may well come up when the panic's over."

"That's the odd thing," said Henry, "the selling starting hours before Antrobus's death. It seems to me he must have been sure that a major scandal was about to come to light. One of his people, a John Sherwood, flew down to Gorsedene early last evening, no doubt to consult with Antrobus on what was to be done."

"I've met Sherwood," Peter told him. "He handles all Antrobus's dirty work. He's a creep."

"Was the selling yesterday general, or did it come from limited sources?"

"According to the rumours, very limited. The story that was going round is that it came chiefly from a small syndicate with an office in Eastcheap. They must have had heavy financial backing, to get sufficient pull with the brokers. And they must have established accounts with quite a lot of brokers over the past few months, so that they could spread the selling."

"Did they deal at all through your firm?"

"Yes. And that's worrying the senior partner more than somewhat. Confidentially, we took on quite a heap from them, not knowing at the time, of course, that they were selling simultaneously through a lot of other brokers. Naturally, they weren't the only sellers. Once the price started dropping, quite a few came in—either professional bears or actual shareholders getting the wind up and unloading."

Henry asked, "Do you know who are in the syndicate?"

"Not offhand. But I could probably find out. Is it significant?"

"It might be."

Peter thought for a minute, then put down his beer. 'There's one chap I could phone. He'll probably have a fair idea. Wait here, old man."

Peter went off to phone. When he returned, he was looking excited.

"You're damn right, Henry. Something very odd indeed. My chum knows something of the history of this syndicate. It was started about fifteen years ago by a few young operators led by a future whizz-kid."

"Not Antrobus himself?"

"Damn right. Antrobus. It was one of his first ventures in the City. To begin with, the syndicate gambled on commodity futures. They had luck. They ran up enough profit in the space of a few months for Antrobus to make his first takeover bid. Since then, nothing much has been heard of this syndicate. It has done a bit of dealing now and then, I gather, but nothing out of the way—until yesterday."

Henry was puzzled. "Antrobus couldn't still have been a member of it."

"My chum says he hadn't been for some time, so far as he knows."

"What does that mean? You make it sound sinister. Oh, come on, Peter. Of course Antrobus couldn't be in on it recently. He'd scarcely be selling his own shares short."

"Why not? If his financial empire was really going to collapse—and who would know better than Antrobus himself?—he might be conducting this bear operation against his own shares, to make a private purse for himself, to take to Brazil or some place before the fireworks started. There are still ways of getting money out of the country in spite of the regulations, especially for a man with his international contacts."

Henry considered. It was possible, of course. But then, why should he hang himself?

"It sounds too wild, Peter. Your friend says Antrobus left that syndicate some years ago. Is there anything at all to connect him with it now?"

Peter Lane picked up his beer and took a swig. "Just one thing, Henry. The story is that there's a chap who organized the whole thing—not officially part of the syndicate itself, but supposed to be master-minding the operation. It's being rumoured that it's John Sherwood."

3

The weather was so warm that the doors and windows of Gorsedene were opened wide. Many of the patients, indeed, had already collected their half-grapefruits and glasses of boiled water in the big front room, and taken them out to savour on the terrace.

When Kate emerged with hers, all the seats around the small tables under the bright parasols seemed to be occupied.

"But there's bound to be a table free soon," she remarked to Bella, who had followed her on to the terrace. "After all, how long can it take to eat half a grapefruit?"

"You'd be surprised, luv. That's the trick. Eat it so slowly that your belly is conned into thinking it's getting fed proper. You take the boiled water in little sips, like a tart in a drawing-room. When it's all gone, you suck the slice of lemon until there's only the ring of peel. Most then eat the peel."

Looking towards the far end of the terrace, Kate saw that Michael Neal was waving to her and pointing to the spare chair at the table which he and his wife had taken.

"Somebody offering me a seat," she told Bella.

"Be seeing you," said Bella affably. "I'd go to sit on the grass, if it wasn't for the ants."

Michael smiled as Kate joined his table, and rose to adjust the parasol to protect the chair for her. Mary was not only sitting in the shade, but was wearing large, dark sunglasses. Her face looked pale, Kate thought, as though she were unwell. But the glasses hid her eyes so completely that one could not tell.

"The secret, Bella tells me," said Kate, carefully digging the first mouthful from her grapefruit, "is to eat this damn thing slowly, as though you were enjoying it."

Michael laughed. "Now she tells me!"

She saw that he had finished his—and that Mary had no plate or bowl in front of her, but only a glass of water.

"Aren't you having any?" Kate asked her. "Good heavens, you'll starve."

"I have a minor stomach upset. So I thought I'd better not indulge."

"From her that hath not shall be taken away even that which she hath," murmured Michael.

Kate smiled. "It's a crying shame."

"I see the Antrobus helicopter is still on the pad," said Michael. Its insect-shape, with the drooping antennae at rest, dominated the view across the lawn to the river. "What's happened to the pilot?"

"He chucked his job and went off by train last evening," Kate told him. "He'd had a row with Antrobus—a personal matter, he said."

"An easy man to have a row with, seemingly," said Michael quietly.

Mary got up. "If you'll excuse me, I think I'll go to my room and lie down for a while. I'm still a little queasy."

"All right, darling. Want me to come?"

"No, I'm all right. I'll feel better resting, that's all. You take your walk."

"Can I get you anything?" asked Kate.

"No thank you. I have some pills the doctor gave me in New York for upsets like this."

"Careful what you take when you're not eating."

"Oh, that'll be all right."

When she had gone, Michael said, "I usually take a walk in the afternoon. How about that? Will you keep me company?"

"I'd like to. Where shall we walk?"

"Alongside the river's pleasantest, I think. We could go as far as the next footbridge and come back on the other side. You get a fine view of Gorsedene from the far bank. Shall we start, if you're ready?"

"Just let me suck the last shred off my lemon peel," said Kate, making a face at the sourness. "Bella advises eating the peel, too, but I don't believe I will. It's a bit sharp. There now, lunch is over. Let's go."

As they walked, he chatted agreeably. He talked of Washington, the gossip of high places. He was a delightful man, civilized, amusing, immensely knowledgeable. The sun was shining, the trees gently bowing in the breeze, the river softly flowing. How enjoyable the walk would have been, if its purpose had not so obviously been prepared by Michael and his wife, the management so evidently staged.

Inevitably he came to it.

"Kate, I'm going to ask you something which sounds a little odd."

"Go ahead."

"Did you mention to the police that you found Mary and myself at Antrobus's door last night?"

"No."

He exhaled with relief. "What was worrying me was that I might be required to testify at the inquest, and that could be adjourned for weeks. I could say nothing that would be of any help, of course."

"Couldn't you?"

For a moment he made no reply. They walked on, side by side, neither looking at the other.

At last he said, with a rueful laugh, "It's having to deal with a newspaperwoman. It's my stupid remark about Antrobus having phoned us to come to his room, isn't it?"

"I knew at once that wasn't true," she told him, still not looking at him. "I'd been trying for some time to phone my husband from my room, but there was no reply from the switchboard. But my phone was in good order; I checked. At first I thought there was no point in checking. Antrobus couldn't have phoned you anyway, because he had been dead for at least an hour. Then I wondered if somebody else might have phoned, and you'd mistaken the voice or something. So I checked. Nobody phoned you, because all that time there was nobody working the Gorsedene switchboard."

"Do you want an explanation?"

"Not unless you want to give me one."

They were approaching a tree that had fallen by the side of the path. He pointed to it. "Let's sit down. You'd better know."

When they were seated on the tree trunk they were at last looking straight at each other.

"Philip Antrobus and I," he began, "had had a difference

of opinion. It was about his company's difficulties with a defence contract in the States. I won't bore you with the details of that. What he wanted was for me to put a few paragraphs in my column that would help him. I refused, and he got angry. Come to think of it, you met us walking right here along the riverside path when we were in the middle of our difference."

Kate nodded. "I thought you both looked heated, but then decided I was imagining things—the distortions of hunger."

He laughed. "We weren't very heated anyway. I simply told him that I would put nothing in my column that was not founded on facts of real interest to my readers.

"He said he had such facts. He gave me an idea of them, and they could have been mildly interesting. But, of course, I wanted more than his word—and he wouldn't even agree to direct attribution. He said he had documents that would substantiate what he told me. They were in his room. I told him that I wasn't sufficiently interested.

"But then, talking it over with Mary late that evening in our room, I began to wonder whether I could get something out of him after all that I could use. So I went to see him. Mary came along because when we're away from Washington she does secretarial chores for me. So she could take a shorthand précis of what Antrobus wanted to show me."

Kate regarded him steadily. "Then why lie about Antrobus phoning you?"

Michael shrugged. "You took me by surprise. I was a little worked-up by the argument I'd been having with the man earlier. So I said the first thing that came into my head. It was stupid. I apologize."

Kate was still regarding him steadily. "When I came out into the corridor, I heard you say to Mary, 'Don't be silly. I have to have it. There are reasons.' "

He did not lower his gaze, but suddenly gave a wry laugh. "The newspaperwoman again."

"I'm not cross-questioning you, Michael. You don't have to explain."

"My dear Kate, there is nothing much to explain. I've

no objection to telling you why I said that, provided it's in confidence, off the record. Because there's another person involved."

"All right."

"I told you that Antrobus wanted me to put some paragraphs in my column that would help him with his defence contract. That was true. But I was not being entirely frank when I added that they could be mildly interesting. They could have been very interesting indeed—in the States, that is, and especially in Washington."

He paused, but Kate said nothing. So he resumed.

"The man chiefly blocking Antrobus's project is a senator of considerable distinction. I won't give you his name, though I suppose you could easily deduce who he is. Your newspaper's diplomatic man would place him in minutes. The senator has an unsullied reputation—in a city where such reputations are not plentiful. What Antrobus claimed to have was documentary proof that the senator was corrupt, that he had taken a very large bribe for a commercial concession.

"I simply did not believe it. He invited me to go to his room and he'd show me the proof. But I refused. Then, during the evening, I talked it over with Mary, as I told you, and I began to think I ought at least to see the evidence.

"So I went along to Antrobus's room. It wasn't really as my secretary that Mary came along. She didn't want me to get involved in the thing at all. She begged me not to touch it. We were still arguing all the way down the corridor, and when we reached his room, she pleaded with me not to go in. Then you saw us, and I was in such a state of indecision that I told that silly lie about the phone, and went away with Mary."

"And the reasons?" asked Kate.

"Very cogent reasons, Kate. There is a possibility, not to put it higher, that this senator—perhaps not next time round, but the time after—could be a strong candidate for the presidency. If there is really a stain of secret corruption, then the sooner it is uncovered the better. If Antrobus could prove what he alleged, he would have got far more than the few paragraphs in my column which he felt were all that was required to remove the obstacle to his plans in the States."

"So now . . . ?"

"I don't know. Now that Antrobus is dead, it'll have to wait until I get back to Washington and I can enquire from other sources."

"Reasons indeed," murmured Kate.

CHAPTER 7

"HE WAS LYING," Kate told Henry.

He had driven back from London in the evening and come round to her room at Gorsedene after he had taken his dinner at the Crown. Kate was in bed. He sat near the window, switching off the television. "Thank you, darling," she said.

Henry considered. "You can only guess that he was lying. You can't be sure."

"But it doesn't add up," she protested. "First there's his admitted lie about a telephone invitation from Antrobus. Why should he react like that when I saw them, if he were simply following up a news story? Then there's all that guff about Mary begging him not to get involved, and arguing all down the corridor, and pleading with him not to go into the room. All so phoney, Henry."

"It does sound improbable," he admitted.

"What I think he was truthful about," she said, "was Senator Galahad. I bet Antrobus was trying to get Michael to put in a few paragraphs maligning the senator—falsely, but mud clings, particularly after all that has happened in Washington these past few years. A hint of scandal from someone as respected as Michael Neal might well make Galahad stop doing whatever Antrobus wanted to stop him doing. Or else, he'd learn, there would be more Neal paragraphs, meatier. All that sounds true."

"But not the allegations themselves, you think?"

"Exactly. I don't think Antrobus could prove anything, or even said that he could. What I guess is that he told Michael to accuse the senator falsely, or Antrobus would publish Heinz Karasak's manuscript about a vice racket still being run by Victor Zucconi's old associates, including possibly his former mistress, this Mary Pastorelli. Antrobus had a publishing house, hadn't he?"

"Yes, and rather that kind of publishing house," Henry admitted.

"He must have had contacts with American publishers of the same kind. So he could easily start an investigation by newspaper reporters into what happened to Mary Pastorelli, and it surely wouldn't be long before Mary Neal's name emerged."

Henry objected that, if Mary Neal really were Zucconi's old girl-friend, some muckraking reporter would have picked up the story when Karasak's original articles on the vice kings were published.

"Not necessarily," reasoned Kate. "They were in a cheap pulp magazine, which nobody pays much attention to, there are so many of them, all full of lies. Then the girl wasn't named in the articles. Indeed, she wasn't even mentioned. There was just that picture—Victor Zucconi and friend. It's in the book that Mary Pastorelli is accused, and more or less convicted. If Antrobus published the book, then dropped a few hints in the right places, he'd soon have somebody linking Mary Pastorelli with Mary Neal."

"But would he?" objected Henry again. "All you're going on is a sort of likeness in a smudged picture."

"That, and the way the Neals behaved. He told me a quite unnecessary lie, he was so shaken at being caught at Antrobus's door. She has been under intense strain ever since I met her. Last night, in that corridor, she looked positively wild with fright."

"Not even good circumstantial."

"But it fits, Henry. Why else should the Neals be here at the same time as Antrobus, unless he was blackmailing them, so they had to come to meet him? Why should Michael have been saying, urgently, that he had to have it? Not simply some evidence about a corrupt senator. All that political stuff he gave me was baloney. If that was all, he'd have told Antrobus to show him the papers, or whatever, next morning—not gone round to his room late at night, desperate to get them. But if it were something that could destroy his wife, on whom he dotes . . . "

"A faint likeness in a smudged picture," Henry reminded her. "That's all you're really going on."

"I'll soon have it positive, one way or the other."

"How?"

"I phoned Butch. He's getting one of our people in New York to find out who Mary Neal was before she married Michael. It shouldn't take a good reporter long."

"Isn't that rather dangerous?" Henry asked. "I mean, if it turns out that she really was Mary Pastorelli?"

"No risk. I know whom Butch is using. He's a perfectly sound, discreet man. He's been told it's a confidential enquiry, not for passing on to anybody, much less for publication. It's okay."

Henry sat in thought for a few moments. Then he said, "You know, on consideration, your whole theory doesn't make sense. Antrobus surely had another copy of that typescript. Neal would certainly have understood that. So getting hold of the typescript wouldn't have made any difference to the threat of blackmail."

"Unless," said Kate slowly, "Michael knew that Antrobus was already dead."

Henry stared at her. "How could he have known? When you saw him, he hadn't even entered the room . . . You mean, he could have been there before? Oh, come on, Kate, stop trying to turn an obvious suicide into murder."

Kate said nothing. She lay back on the pillow, gazing at the ceiling.

Henry laughed. "If you want to make it murder, I can give you a much better candidate for murderer."

He told her of his afternoon in London, and of what he had learned from Peter Lane about the bear raid.

"This syndicate," he concluded, "was clearly working to a carefully-laid plan. It couldn't have been put together hurriedly in a few hours. For one thing, the syndicate must have spent months quietly cultivating several stockbrokers, to be able to make a big raid without rousing instant suspicion. Now, who do you think is said to be the grey eminence behind the syndicate? John Sherwood."

Kate jerked up in bed; then lay down again slowly,

murmuring, "I shouldn't have done that. Any sudden movement brings on a dizzy spell."

"You're all right?" he asked anxiously.

"Yes, darling. Just a little weak, from lack of food. Go on with your theory."

He smiled, indulging her. "All right. So this syndicate knows, months in advance, that there's going to be a certain day on which they can make their raid, because they know that Antrobus will die that same night, and his shares therefore plummet next morning. The syndicate couldn't possibly know, of course, that Antrobus would hang himself on a particular night. So, the raid having been made, the shares sold short, John Sherwood flew down here last evening and somehow managed to hang Antrobus by the neck to that pipe in the bathroom. How's that for a theory? As good as yours, anyhow."

Kate raised herself again from the pillow, but slowly this time, eyes half closed, muttering, "Steady. Steady. That's better."

When she was sitting upright, she opened her eyes at Henry.

"Darling, I've just remembered. About ten minutes before I found the Neals in the corridor last night, I'd gone to the door of my room to ask a passerby if he knew where the coinbox phone booth was. He said very rudely that he didn't. It was John Sherwood, and I had the impression that he had just left Antrobus's room."

Henry laughed quietly. "Now, instead of one simple suicide, we have not one, but two murderers." He rose and kissed her gently. "I'm off to the hotel. Try to get some sleep, darling. There are things to be sorted out in this business. There's been a lot of dirty work. But not murder, Kate dear. Not murder."

When he had gone, Kate dozed. Half an hour later she opened her eyes sharply and reached for the phone. Lal was on the switchboard. She asked him to get through to her husband at the Crown.

"Henry, I've just thought of something. Are you in bed?"

"No. I'm in the phone booth in the hall. I was in the bar having a whisky."

"Oh hell!"

"What is it?" he asked. "Is it the mysterious something you knew you had seen that was wrong, but couldn't place?"

"No. I'm sure there was something wrong, but I still can't place it. This is something else. A question, really. The doors on all these rooms are fitted with locks that are self-locking. Why was Philip Antrobus's door open?"

"I suppose because he opened it. Go to sleep, darling. I'll come round in the morning, and we can talk and theorize as much as you like."

"Don't come before twelve. I'm to have my underwater massage. And they say it takes it out of one. But there's still this question. It follows in a way the question that started me wondering—if you were going to kill yourself, would you first go on a health cure?

"Now the next question. If you were going to hang yourself, would you leave the door open so that anybody could walk in?"

CHAPTER 8

THE UNDERWATER MASSAGE was indeed exhausting. As Kate lay back in the large, warm bath, her head supported on a leather strap, she prepared to relax. But the turbulence, the pummelling at every muscle, the pulsation, once the machine started, would admit no such luxury. Thankfully Mavis, operating the thing, said little. No doubt she knew that patients undergoing this particular treatment had no energy for chatter. Kate was mightily relieved when the girl eventually shut the action off, and grateful for the arm that helped her out of the bath.

"I was warned it was tiring," she said.

Mavis smiled sympathetically. "Everybody finds that, madam, even the men. It doesn't matter how strong you are. But it's the finest massage you can get, the most modern method. It's wonderful for toning up the system, and it gets the weight down."

"Well, thank heavens for that."

"After a few treatments, you get quite used to it."

"I doubt if I'll make the attempt."

When Kate was dressed, she took a deckchair out into the sunshine on the front lawn. She lay back in the chair, limp. Undoubtedly it was a wonderful machine, but she would not try it again, she promised herself. A side effect, she was now discovering, was to revive the pangs of hunger that she thought she had stifled.

She found herself craving food even more urgently than she had on the first two days. At that moment, she idly mused, she would eagerly sacrifice her immortal soul for a herring baked in breadcrumbs, or a large pork pie. If there had been underwater massage in Chris Marlowe's day, she fancied, Mephistopheles would not have tempted Faustus with Helen of Troy. A fillet steak with onion rings and French-fried potatoes would have sufficed. Or Boeuf Stroganoff, she thought, lovingly, or better still Bourguignonne, and on the side a potato baked in its jacket, well buttered.

A shadow darkened her eyelids. She opened them to see Bella smiling down at her.

"Had the underwater stuff, eh?" asked Bella. "Takes it out of you proper, don't it?"

She was carrying a deckchair, which she unfolded and set alongside Kate's.

Since politeness forbade dozing off again, Kate said, "Weren't you going to tell me about that dinner you had on Philip Antrobus's motor cruiser?"

Bella chuckled. "You'd not credit it, luv."

"I'll try."

After a pause, Bella started: "Okay, then. Summer night it was—raining, of course, but warm. There was about a dozen of us. I knew a couple of the men, who played in one of the groups, but none of the girls. But you could tell what they was, just looking at 'em. Classy whores, the Mayfair sort with luxury pads around Shepherd Market, and never so much as taking their knickers off for less than fifty quid. You know the kind."

"I've heard tell," said Kate, amused.

"Kneeboots, a couple of 'em was wearing. Well, when I saw that lot, I almost quit the date before it started. We was getting on this motor cruiser at that little pier near Westminster Bridge. Philip himself was doing the driving, and one of the men dishing out the booze. Champagne, scotch, gin—whatever you wanted. Couple of the girls started giggling before we got as far as Putney. So then one of the fellows from the group got out a guitar and started to sing, and then they all got singing, and—well, you know the sort of party."

"Been to a few," admitted Kate.

"I could see it was going to get rough, luv. But I didn't guess how rough."

"What sort of rough?"

Bella shook her head reminiscently. "There was a lot more drinking, and a few things to eat—nice things, smoked salmon, oysters and all that . . ."

"Don't," begged Kate.

Bella grinned. "After a bit, one of the other blokes took over the driving, and Philip started messing about with one of the girls. The other blokes were getting at them, too. One tried it on me, but I told him where to stick it. 'I'm here to sing,' I says. 'Then sing, bugger you,' says he. So I sing, and the guitar player picks it up, and we gets in a corner and has music. Nobody else paid no attention. Busy, they was. Well, then the driver pulled the boat up by some little island in the river. We was a long way up the river by then, and it was dark and lonely. I was a bit scared, because the party was getting real dirty."

"How?" asked Kate.

For a while Bella said nothing. Then she went on slowly, reluctantly, "By then most of 'em was pretty pissed. Not Philip, he wasn't. He drunk as much as any, but he never seemed to feel it."

"How dirty?" asked Kate again.

"Well, some of 'em was stripping out, and the men pulling the girls' dresses off and all that. And then one of the men brought out a little silky whip. So there was a girl with nothing on by then except her kneeboots. So another fellow grabbed her and held her against the table while the first fellow beat her."

"Beat her properly?"

"Not too hard, but not playing at it either. Then, sudden, Philip gets all excited. Real wild, he looked. Eyes flashing and all that, and wet round the mouth.

"He chucks off his jacket and pulls off his shirt. Then he grabs the whip and hands it to the girl in the boots. She was all flushed and wild, too.

"'Come on,' he says. And he stands himself up against the wall and she starts hitting him. She wasn't playing at it neither. Getting her own back, if you ask me.

"So I says to the guitar player, 'Time we left here, George.'

"'How?' says he.

"'We'll find some way,' says I.

"So we goes up on deck. Very dark it was, and nobody about, no other boats. Good way along the river bank there was a light in a house, but nothing nearer, and it was still raining.

" 'We could get on that island,' I says to George.

" 'There's nothing there except swans,' says he, 'and it'd be bloody cold all night.'

"Then he looks at the back, and there's a little rowing boat tied on, bobbing about in the water. So George pulls it alongside, and helps me in. There wasn't no oars. I told him to use his guitar, but he said not bloody likely, and he starts paddling with his hands.

"Anyway, the river was going pretty fast, and took us along. Then there was a bend, so we was near the bank, and George grabbed hold of some tree hanging out over the water, and we got ashore. We were in this field of cabbages or some muck. But in the end we got on a road, and walked till we found a pub, and then George phoned for a taxi, and we got back to London. Cost me quids, the taxi did. But worth it. I never wants that sort of party again, I'm telling you, luv."

"The English vice, that's what the French call it, flagellation," murmured Kate.

"Flajee-what?"

Kate smiled. "Whipping for sexual pleasure. The English vice."

"Not the English I knows," said Bella firmly.

"No," agreed Kate. "A rich man's sport."

It would be something interesting, she thought lazily, to tell Henry. It would shock him badly. He shocked easily. And he looked so comic, and very adorable, when he was shocked.

2

When she had eaten her midday half-grapefruit and thus gained sufficient strength, Kate went up to her room and phoned her newspaper.

"Kate Theobald here. Put me through to Butch, please . . . Hallo, Butch . . . Yes, darling, positively svelte. Now listen, Butch, can you look up a few things for me in the library? . . . I want some history stuff of Philip Antrobus . . . Well, there may just be a story . . . No, I'm not talking about it, not yet. Perhaps not at all. Maybe there isn't one."

"What sort of story?" he asked. "I've arranged to cover the inquest on Friday. What else is there?"

"Probably nothing."

"All right, Kate. Play it your way. What information do you want?"

"First, a list of all Philip Antrobus's companies. Can do?"

"I suppose so. Antrobus Enterprises is a holding company—and judging by today's price in the market, well and truly down the drain. Our City office will know what companies it holds. What do you want to know about them?"

"Just the name of each and, very briefly, what it does. Could you put that in the post for me to Gorsedene, so that I get it tomorrow morning?"

"Very well. Anything else?"

"I want to know who the women are whom Philip Antrobus was mixed up with since he made his dough—the playboy stuff. It'll be in the cuttings."

"It'll practically fill his cuttings," said Butch.

"I want just the steadies," she told him. "Not the one-night stands. Women he was linked with for a few months or, at any rate, a few weeks. Especially, I want to know about his association with his wife before they married, and with two other women in particular."

"Who are?"

"Janet Dimpsey, the wife of the director here. I think she may have known Antrobus before she was married, but I don't know her maiden name. I expect you can dig that out. The other is Bella."

"The pop queen? Kate, what are you up to?"

"I don't really know. It'll probably come to nothing. It's astonishing, the hallucinations you get from hunger."

Butch laughed. "By the way, I've got the report from Willy in New York. Michael Neal's wife was a girl named Mary Pastorelli. They were married just over three years ago in a small, rather obscure town in Canada—in

Ontario, actually. Her address was given as Chicago. Rather oddly, there was no publicity. After the marriage, they flew to Europe for a few weeks—honeymoon, I suppose. Then Neal arrived back in Washington with his new wife. It was assumed that they'd met and married in Europe. Willy thinks that tale was actually put around, and nobody thought to question it. He had quite a job, tracing the Canadian marriage. Rather slick of him, I thought.

"You mentioned an author named Heinz Karasak who might be able to help him. But Willy found that Karasak —who seems to have been a tired old newspaper hack— died a couple of months ago. What's the point of all this, Kate?"

"I don't know yet. Maybe there'll be none, as I keep on telling you. Could be just feminine curiosity. You'll get me those clippings, won't you, Butch, and the information about the companies?"

"All right, though it sounds like a waste of time."

"Probably," she assured him cheerfully, and rang off.

There was a knock on her door. She opened to Henry.

"How was the underwater massage?"

"Exhausting. I've spent most of the time since sitting listless in the sun. But with a diversion."

She told him of Bella and the party on the Thames. Henry made a little grimace of disgust.

"That interview with Philip Antrobus I did for the *Post*," she said, "turns out not to have been in much depth."

"I don't know why you're bothering about the fellow. He was almost certainly a crook, and quite certainly a bastard, and he hanged himself—commendably, I'd say, if it weren't for what it has done to the stock market."

"Bad?"

"Knocked it sideways. I was talking to Peter on the phone just before I came here. Not far short of a market crash, he said.

"He added, by the way, that the syndicate that made the bear raid on Antrobus Enterprises, if it was on the scale he thinks it was, must have made as much as a couple of million pounds. His firm handled some of their transactions. They've been buying Antrobus shares at not much more than one-third of what they sold them short for on Monday."

"John Sherwood left here yesterday," she told him. "He stayed only on Monday night, to confer with Antrobus. He wasn't here as a patient. I suppose he went back to London to collect the loot."

"He'll have to wait a week. It's that long to settling day."

"Then surely they can stop the syndicate getting away with it."

"Damn difficult," said Henry. "If the Stock Exchange really thought there was a leak from inside the Antrobus organization that inspired the selling, they could freeze the transactions—if they weren't so occupied with everything else that they had time to bother with it.

"But then they'd have to establish the leak. Sherwood has no traceable connection with the syndicate, you can bet on that. The syndicate members would simply say that they had been studying Antrobus Enterprises and decided they were shaky, so they had carried out a bear operation, expecting modest gains. It was the Antrobus suicide, which of course they could not have foretold, that magnified the gains so enormously. I can't see the deals being cancelled after an enquiry, because Antrobus Enterprises must in fact have been very shaky indeed, to lead Antrobus to kill himself."

"If he did kill himself," she murmured.

Henry laughed. "Your famous theory. Or was it mine? The syndicate sold the shares short on Monday afternoon, and John Sherwood came here on Monday evening to murder his boss. That is, he somehow managed to overcome a normally healthy and active man, and string him up by a dressing-gown cord to a pipe in his bathroom, without a struggle or any disturbance which you would have heard in the next-door room. Turn it in, Kate. What do you do here in the afternoon? Do you want to rest? Shall I go?"

"I was thinking of taking a walk."

"I'll come with you," he volunteered. "Where shall we go?"

"Along the river bank is pleasantest."

3

As they emerged on to the front lawn, they saw a young man in a leather jerkin climbing into the helicopter; a few moments later its engine opened up.

"That's not the original pilot," said Kate. "They must have sent him down to collect it. Charles Pugh chucked up his job on Monday evening, and went back to London by train."

"Charles Pugh—was that his name?" Henry asked. "Then he didn't return to London by train on Monday evening."

"How do you know?"

"From the landlord of the Crown. He's a bit worried. It seems that Pugh arrived at the Crown with a bag earlyish on Monday evening, booked a room, put his bag in, and went to dinner in the pub's dining-room. By then the evening train to London had gone. After dinner, Pugh went out, and didn't return. His bag was still there next day. And, of course, he hadn't paid his bill. The landlord thought he'd been conned out of the price of a dinner, and asked me last night whether he ought to open the bag to see what it contains. I advised him not to, but to call in the local police."

"Sergeant Grey. That won't get him far."

"Anyway, it turned out not to matter," Henry went on. "This morning the landlord had a phone call from London, instructing him to send the bag, and his bill, to the Antrobus office."

The rotors of the helicopter were now turning. Kate and Henry stood and watched as, a few minutes later, the machine lifted from the pad and scurried away.

"Where do you think Charles Pugh went?" asked Kate.

Henry chuckled. "Maybe he returned to Gorsedene and hanged Philip Antrobus."

Kate stared at him. "Why should he?"

"To make a guess at that, I'd have to know why Pugh chucked up his job."

"I know that," Kate said. "He told me. Personal reasons."

Henry was laughing. "There you are, then. Obviously there was a strong motive, though we don't happen to know precisely what. How many putative murderers have you got now, darling? Three, isn't it? John Sherwood, in order to make his fortune on the Stock Exchange; Charles Pugh, for unknown but probably imperative personal reasons; and Michael Neal, to stop Antrobus blackmailing him over his wife. You pays your money and, as the old phrase goes, you takes your choice. All good, sound theories, each as likely (or as unlikely) as the others—if you exclude the rather better one that Philip Antrobus killed himself."

"Henry darling," she said, "I wish you'd kindly remember that I've had practically nothing to eat, and no single drop of alcohol, for three days. And sarcasm is likely to make me suddenly burst out crying."

"Sorry. But they are somewhat wild phantasies."

"All right, Henry. But there are oddities. For instance, I don't for a moment think that Michael Neal really murdered Philip Antrobus. But there's little doubt that Antrobus was blackmailing him, trying to compel him to write something false in his column, under the threat of exposing his wife. She was Mary Pastorelli before she married him. Butch has had that checked. They got married very quietly in a small town in Ontario, and the marriage was carefully hushed. So it is odd, isn't it?"

"Perhaps. But irrelevant. The plain fact is, Kate, that Antrobus killed himself because of the financial disaster that hit his company, and probably because he knew that, in consequence, a fraud would come to light that would inevitably lead to a prison sentence."

"And there's another odd thing," mused Kate. Henry understood that she had not been listening. "I don't really think for a moment that Charles Pugh came back to Gorsedene that evening and killed Philip Antrobus. I expect he met somebody, or something happened, that made him change his plan to stay in the Crown that night. Perhaps somebody gave him a lift in a car. But whatever the reason he left, why didn't he go back to the Crown to pick up his bag?"

"There must have been a reason. Probably something quite ordinary."

"And, Henry, he had had a row with Philip Antrobus

and turned in his job. So how did anyone at Antrobus Enterprises know he had left his bag and an unpaid bill at the Crown?"

"Presumably Pugh told them, and asked them to settle up for him."

"But why should they? He had left them in a furious temper. I should have thought they'd be the last people he'd ask, if he couldn't simply pick up his bag and his bill himself."

"Isn't it rather futile," he asked, "to frame imaginary questions, without any knowledge at all of the facts?"

"You're always so practical and level-headed, Henry," she complained. "It's rather boring. My questions are much more fun."

4

After they had walked for quite a short distance along the river bank, she asked him to turn back. She was more tired, physically, than she had thought she was. Henry was solicitous, and a little worried. All this health cure nonsense—he hoped it was not doing her actual harm.

Not at all, she assured him. She would emerge at the end of the week fitter than she had been for years and, what was much more important, slimmer.

"But the regimen is exhausting, there's no denying that. Let's turn back through the woods. You can have a cup of tea with me on the terrace, and then go back to the Crown, and I'll go to my room to rest. Sorry about folding up on you. But you've got the usual pub things at the Crown, and I dare say the local lads in the public bar will give you a game of darts."

"I brought a couple of briefs with me," he reminded her, "and a few of the necessary books. I could do with a few hours without interruptions."

As they returned through the woods, she told him of the three Indians she had come across on her last walk that way, and laughed as she admitted she had been scared at what she took to be gibberish voices. This time the woods were empty.

They crossed the golf fairway, and she led him through the vast vegetable garden.

"Over there are the kitchens, darling, where all that delicious water is boiled."

She showed him the gymnasium, the billiards room, the squash courts. She led him past the riding stables where several girls were just dismounting. A stable hand was lowering sacks of feed from the grain store above, another receiving them on the ground. This second man hastened to take the horses from the riders, leading them off into the stalls.

"If it weren't full of cranks, and empty of food and drink," said Henry genially, "this'd be rather a good place for a holiday."

When they had drunk tea on the front terrace, she told him to leave. She would go up to her room and look at the telly. "It's just about time for the children's programmes—about the right intellectual level for dieters. I'll ring you in the morning."

She was glad to get to her room and rest for an hour on the bed. She had a portable radio, so she switched on for the news; but then switched off again. The news, as always, so depressing—and anyway she was having a holiday from all that.

She dozed for a while, then lay with her eyes open, retracing so far as she could remember the sounds she had heard from Antrobus's room that Monday evening.

First the argument with a woman; but which woman, and about what? Then, later, the laughter dimly heard. Later still, that curious tapping noise, and the thud.

At that precise moment she heard the thud again.

It was so apt she almost screamed with fright. Then she pulled herself together and listened. The thud had come from Antrobus's room. Of that she was sure. Yet who was there? The room was securely locked. She had ascertained that from Lal. Mr. Antrobus's business documents and his other possessions were still there, he had told her. So the room had to be securely locked.

It had not been a loud noise. Kate tried to decide whether it had been as loud as, or similar to, the thud she had heard on Monday evening. But she had to admit to herself that she simply did not know. Her recollections were only vague, sleepy.

It was too much for her curiosity. She rose from her bed and went out into the corridor.

The door of the next room was shut. There was nobody in the corridor. She stepped over to the door and gently turned the handle.

The door opened.

With a little gasp of wonder at her bravery, she pushed it wider, and went in.

A lamp was lit on the table where Philip Antrobus's wallets of business papers had been piled; the heavy curtains were drawn across the windows, so that the light would not show outside.

A chair upon which some of the wallets had evidently been placed had toppled over backwards. The thud!

Several of the wallets lay where they had fallen on the floor. From a couple which had burst open the documents had been scattered across the carpet.

A woman was kneeling among them, picking up a paper to examine. She held it in her hand as, at Kate's entrance, she looked up towards her.

It was Phoebe Sadler.

CHAPTER 9

AFTER HENRY HAD put in a couple of hours' work in his room on the more complicated of the briefs, he felt in need of a drink. At the bottom of the stairs he was stopped by Jerry Toomey, the landlord of the Crown. "Could I have a word with you, Mr. Theobald?"

"Of course."

The landlord looked round uneasily. "In my office, sir?"

He led the way into his small office, the desk piled with letters and bills pinned into bulldog grips, the walls enlivened with the nudes of the gift calendars favoured by soft-drinks manufacturers.

"It's seeing as you're a lawyer, Mr. Theobald. I need your advice."

"Strictly, you should talk to your solicitor."

"I would normally, sir. But this is different. There's a policeman here, arrived this afternoon. He wanted to see what was in the bag that Mr. Pugh left behind."

"Did you check his credentials?"

"Oh, yes. He's a policeman all right. He had his identification, photo and all, properly stamped. I'm familiar with police identification. Have to be, in my business. He's a Detective Chief Superintendent Norman Stoddart, and he's from Scotland Yard."

"Did you let him have the bag? I take it that you hadn't yet sent it off to the Antrobus office in London."

"Not yet. I'd arranged for the carrier to pick it up tomorrow morning. Our local carrier does a London run once a week, every Thursday. Seemed the easiest way to send it. Yes, I let the officer have the bag. What else could I do, Mr. Theobald?"

"You could have refused. In fact, I think you would

have been wiser to refuse. However, it's done now. Did he give you a receipt for it?"

Toomey shook his head uneasily.

"Would you like me to have a quiet word with him?" asked Henry.

"Oh yes, please, if you would, Mr. Theobald. I'm dead worried. He's in the bar."

The Chief Superintendent was seated on a settle near the window, with a pewter tankard on the table before him. At that early hour there was nobody else in the bar, and the landlord's wife, busy with preparations for dinner, was looking in only occasionally to see if drinks were wanted.

Stoddart was a tall, thin man with a good-humoured face. But shrewd, Henry assessed. The best approach would be the direct, open one.

"Good evening, Chief Superintendent. My name's Theobald. Mr. Toomey, the landlord, has asked me to have a word with you."

"As a lawyer, Mr. Theobald?" He smiled at Henry's look of surprise. "I was talking to Mr. Peter Lane, the stockbroker, this morning. When he heard I was coming here, he told me you'd be at the local pub. He was pretty sure you wouldn't be staying at the health farm with Mrs. Theobald. Too fond of your comforts, Mr. Lane said."

Henry smiled in return. "Too true. So that's how you knew I'm a lawyer."

"Oh no, sir. I've seen you in court. Crichton versus Taylor, the case was. I sat through it all."

"You did? But why? Wait a minute, I've got it. It was a civil action, but there was a hint it might lead to an indictment for fraud. But it never did."

"We never had quite enough on the gentleman to bring a charge. But it was fraud all right."

"Are you on the Fraud Squad?"

"Attached, sir, as you might say."

"Talking of comforts," said Henry, "I was about to get myself a drink. Can I get you one at the same time? What is it, bitter?" He crossed to the bar. "Two pints please, Mrs. Toomey."

When he and the policeman had settled with their beer,

Henry asked, "Is it on suspicion of a fraud that you've come here?"

Stoddart said nothing.

"Since you went to Peter Lane," Henry proceeded, "it's not difficult to guess the area of the suspected fraud. I take it, the bear raid on Monday on Antrobus Enterprises. Peter handled some of the sales for that syndicate."

"He said he had told you about that," agreed Stoddart.

"Come now, Mr. Stoddart, don't be coy. I'm a barrister. I shan't betray any police secrets. But I should like to be able to reassure the landlord about Charles Pugh's valise. You weren't entitled to it, of course, unless you have authority from a magistrate. I'm sure you haven't, or you'd have shown it to him."

"The bag will be returned to Mr. Toomey this evening, sir."

"With all its contents? Not quite all, eh? Wouldn't that look a little awkward, if it came out?"

Again the policeman said nothing.

"Anyway," Henry went on, "what had Charles Pugh to do with any alleged fraud by the syndicate? He was the Antrobus helicopter pilot, that's all."

"Do you know where Mr. Pugh went, sir?"

"No idea. In fact, I've never met him. My wife has, briefly, at Gorsedene. He was having a row with Antrobus, she gathered, and throwing up his job, for personal reasons. He told the porter to get him a taxi to take him to the station after his interview with Antrobus. That's all I know, except of course that he changed his mind, and took a room here for the night instead of going on the train. But you know about all that."

The policeman nodded: "That, and a bit more."

"I'm not trying to be difficult," said Henry. "Getting that valise from the landlord was quite irregular. But if you can show me that it was important, in the interests of justice, I'll simply return the valise to Mr. Toomey, and forget that I know anything at all about its contents. But I have to be convinced, Mr. Stoddart."

The policeman was taking his pipe out of his pocket, busying himself with the tobacco, holding a match to it, puffing carefully until he had got it going to his satisfaction, before looking again at Henry.

"Fair enough, Mr. Theobald," he said at last, "provided that what I tell you is completely off the record, and officially we've never had this conversation."

"No promises. But go ahead."

So the policeman started: "You naturally thought, when I told you that I had been to see Mr. Lane, that I was concerned with what happened in Stock Exchange dealings last Monday. But that was not what I was after, though it may come into the picture in time. We follow up any activity by that syndicate, because for several years we've been looking into a suspected fraud—a very large fraud—carried out shortly after the syndicate was first formed by Philip Antrobus and his jackal, a man named John Sherwood."

"I've not met Sherwood," said Henry, "but I know his reputation."

"I won't bother you with details of the fraud we suspect. It was largely a company-promoting operation, and there was a currency side to it, too. In fact, a much smaller fraud did come to light at the time, and a prosecution was brought, not against the syndicate but against only one member of it. We didn't suspect the major fraud until some years afterwards, and we've been investigating it quietly ever since then. As you know, Mr. Theobald, fraud investigations can drag on for years. As this one has. What we are pretty sure of is that the minor fraud was only the tip of the iceberg, as you might say, and the major fraud would have been suspected very much earlier if that man had ever been brought to trial."

"He scarpered?"

"In a sense. Two days before he was to up on remand before the Bow Street magistrate, he shot himself. Anyway, that was the inquest verdict—suicide while the balance of his mind was disturbed. His name was Leonard Pugh. He was Charles Pugh's father."

Henry whistled softly. "So that was the personal reason for Charles Pugh to have a blazing row with Antrobus and throw up his job. But why only now, Mr. Stoddart?"

"That's just the point. We've known of Charles Pugh all along, of course, but we never went near him. He was a child at the time of his father's death, and could have known nothing of the circumstances. If we'd carried out our enquiries in that direction we might well have scared off the men we were chiefly after."

"Antrobus?"

Stoddart nodded. "And his jackal. If they had got that sort of hint, they'd have covered every possible approach beyond discovery. They're a clever lot. But when the news came—in your wife's newspaper report—of Antrobus's death, I got into touch with the local police and learned that Charles Pugh had had a row with Antrobus and chucked up his job. Sergeant Grey knew of it because the helicopter stood idle on the lawn at Gorsedene and he asked what had happened to the pilot. Apparently everybody knew about the row."

"In that sort of place," said Henry, "everybody knows about everything in five minutes."

"Sure. But then an odd thing happened. Pugh's house, in a London suburb, was broken into last night, though nothing much seems to have been taken."

"Coincidence?"

"Perhaps. Anyway, I then decided to approach young Pugh, and came down here to find him. I didn't know, until I got to the Crown, that he had gone off and left his valise behind. That was when I thought I should have a look into that bag. Are you satisfied, Mr. Theobald?"

"What did you find?"

The policeman hesitated, put a match to his pipe, fussed with it until he had got it drawing well again, then looked at Henry and smiled.

"Very well. After Leonard Pugh's death, Antrobus made his widow an allowance—quite a generous one. She was a simple sort of woman, knew nothing of business, just a wife and mother. Antrobus also paid for the boy's education, then his flying training, after which he gave him the job of helicopter pilot to the firm."

"So?"

"Two weeks ago Mrs. Pugh died. Inoperable cancer. The son decided to sell what had been the family house ever since his parents married, and move into a service flat. In going through the house, he must have come across a store of his father's old business papers, which no doubt Mrs. Pugh had stoved into a trunk and left in the loft. The son went through the papers carefully—must have done. Among them he found copious notes his father had made in preparation for evidence he proposed to give at his trial. Of course, I can't be sure exactly how Charles found those notes made by his father long ago, but it was probably something like that."

"It's the notes you have extracted from the valise?" asked Henry.

"Just so."

"They involve Antrobus?"

"Antrobus, John Sherwood, and a couple more who were then in the syndicate. Involve them good and proper, Mr. Theobald. It's the evidence I've been looking for for about three years."

Henry said, "You think that whoever broke into Pugh's house in London last night was looking for those notes?"

"Possibly."

Henry considered. "It seems rather odd about the notes themselves. If Leonard Pugh was going to spill the beans at his trial, why did he shoot himself? He could have turned Queen's evidence, and might have got away with it."

"Who can tell," said the detective, "after all this time? My guess is that, in the end, he couldn't face it. Even if he escaped a prison sentence, his life would be ruined, he would be disgraced, his family destitute. He might even have bargained with Antrobus—offered silence, irreversible silence, for a promise to keep his wife and son in comfort. I don't know. I don't suppose we shall ever know. Are you satisfied, Mr. Theobald?"

"Give me the valise to return to Toomey," said Henry. "I know nothing whatever about the contents."

2

Toomey was very relieved to get that valise back. Henry took it to him in his office.

"That copper wouldn't give it to me, Mr. Theobald. Just shows what a lawyer can do, sir."

Henry laughed. "I think he was going to give it back to you anyway. He just wanted to have a look at what it contained."

Toomey was reaching for a bottle of scotch from a corner cupboard. "You'll join me in a drink, sir?"

"A small one, thank you, Mr. Toomey. I've some work to do this evening on a brief—getting ready for a case when the courts reopen for Michaelmas."

Handing him the drink, Toomey asked, "What did he want to look into Mr. Pugh's bag for, then?"

"No idea," said Henry. "Well, cheers. Then I must get ready for dinner. What is Mrs. Toomey giving us tonight?"

"Tomato soup, roast pork and apple tart."

"I must be careful not to tell my wife. It'd drive her up the wall."

The landlord smiled. "Lot of damn nonsense, eh, that starving lark up at Gorsedene? Still, it's good for trade."

"Your trade?" asked Henry, surprised.

Toomey winked. "Lots of 'em sneak out down here of an evening. Smoked salmon sandwiches they usually want, that sort of thing. And I keep a good stock of Mumm Cordon Rouge."

Henry marvelled. "Fancy paying all that money to starve for your health, then cheating yourself. They must be crazy."

"Cranky, anyhow," agreed Toomey. "Of course, not your missus. No offense meant."

"And none taken," Henry dutifully assured him, getting up. "Roast pork and apple tart, eh? I must go and wash."

When he reached the dining-room he looked around for Stoddart, but the policeman was not there, nor did he appear.

Henry asked Toomey what had happened to him.

"He went back to London by the evening train. There's a diner on that one, and he said he'd get something to eat on the way."

The brief Henry was studying meant concentrated reading. He sat by the open window of his bedroom. The moon was clouded over, the night dark, but warm. After a couple of hours his attention was slipping. He went down to the bar for a nightcap. The bar was crowded, not only with locals, but with a party of men and women at one end round a couple of champagne buckets. Toomey winked at Henry. Gorsedene patients playing truant.

Henry took a scotch and soda, sipping it slowly while Toomey called out his request for "Last orders, please. Last orders, gents, if you please." He and Mrs. Toomey were still frantically serving them when Henry finished his drink and went up to bed. That pork had been good and solid, and now he was feeling sleepy.

What woke him was the dog barking. It was kennelled in the yard behind the pub. He switched on his bedside lamp and looked at his watch. It was two o'clock in the morning.

Blast the dog, he thought. He was reaching to dowse the light when he heard footsteps in the passage outside.

He went to his door. The light from his room showed Toomey, in a nightshirt—heaven's sake, a nightshirt!—just about to descend the stairs. Over his arm he carried a shotgun.

"What's up?" asked Henry.

The landlord raised his finger to his lips, and whispered, "That dog don't bark for nothing. I'm going down to see."

"I'll come with you," whispered Henry, pulling on his dressing-gown.

Toomey had a flashlight which he shone cautiously around the entrance hall at the foot of the stairs. Nobody there.

Henry followed him quietly down the stairs.

Pointing to the door to the bar, Toomey whispered, "We'd a good night tonight. There's nigh on a hundred and fifty pounds in that till."

Henry touched him on the shoulder. "You stand ready with the gun. I'll open the door."

He crept over to the door, flattening himself against the wall while he gently turned the handle. Then he pushed the door open.

Toomey came forward fast, gun ready. He switched on

the light. There was nobody in the bar. He hastened to the till, pulled it open and saw with relief that it was still stuffed with money.

"What was the dog making all that fuss for, then?" he wondered.

"He has stopped now," said Henry. "But we'd better have a look around."

Toomey went first, switching on lights as they came to them. They went through the dining-room and out into the kitchen. Everything seemed in order. Toomey tried the door to the cellar. It was locked.

"Better have a look down there, all the same," suggested Henry.

Toomey was reaching above the lintel where he hid the key. Henry followed the landlord down the flight of stone steps. The cellar was stacked with barrels of beer, crates of spirits, the walls lined with well-filled racks of wine.

"Everything in order?" asked Henry.

"Seems to be," muttered Toomey, puzzled. "I can't understand that dog."

They came up from the cellar. There remained only Toomey's office.

He switched on the light, then gasped and pointed at the window. It was open. Henry stepped across to examine it.

"Been forced with a jemmy," he told Toomey.

The latter was standing by his desk, bewildered, turning over the papers stacked upon it, opening the drawers.

"I don't get it," he said. "There's nothing much in here to take, nothing of any value. And I can't see that anything's been touched anyway. Maybe he broke in and then got scared when the dog started up, and bolted."

Suddenly Henry asked, "Where did you put Mr. Pugh's bag?"

"Over there in the corner . . ."

He broke off, staring at the corner.

"It's gone."

3

When Phoebe Sadler looked up, at Kate's entrance, from where she was kneeling on the floor of Antrobus's room, a document in her hand, both women were motionless and silent for a few moments.

Then Phoebe smiled. "Hallo, there."

"Hallo," Kate uncertainly responded.

"If you're coming in, shut the door. And I don't want to be interrupted again, so drop the latch. I thought I had, but I must have fumbled it."

Kate shut the door behind her and released the catch on the lock.

"How did you get in?" she asked.

"Borrowed a key from Pelham."

Kate, wondering why Pelham Dimpsey had let her have the key, offered, "I'm in the next room. The walls are thin. I heard a thud. I suppose it was that chair."

"It fell over when I put too many of these damn briefcases on it. Careless of me." She smiled again. "I suppose you want to know what I'm doing here."

"No business of mine," admitted Kate, "but out of curiosity . . ."

"I'm looking for Philip's life-insurance policy." She held up the document in her hand. "And I've just found it. I haven't had time to read it. You interrupted."

Kate suddenly understood. Her mind flashed back to Pelham Dimpsey talking to the newspaper reporters. He and his wife, he had said, had known Phoebe and Philip Antrobus for many years. Phoebe.

"You're his wife."

Phoebe got up from the floor. "I was until we divorced. If we hadn't, I'd now be his widow."

She sat in one of the armchairs and motioned Kate to another.

"Then Mr. Dimpsey must know who you are," said Kate, "and that you're here."

"Of course he does. He arranged it."

"Did your husband—or rather, Mr. Antrobus—know that you'd be here?"

"Yes. My dear, there's no mystery about it. We had the divorce, thank God. Philip was an absolute bastard. I won't go into details. But so rich! It makes me sigh to think of it, even now.

"Still, there was no real alternative to the divorce. Our

lawyers settled the money side of it. The dispute was Rosabel—our daughter. She's only three years old.

"Philip wanted to keep her and, since technically he was divorcing me, he stood a good chance. The arrangement is you go before a judge in chambers. We've been once. Frightening, my dear, but comfortingly private. No bloody reporters—oh, sorry, I forgot. This isn't for your newspaper, is it?"

Kate shook her head. "Even if I wanted to, I couldn't. It would be contempt of court, and I'd go down for a stretch. Or perhaps the editor would, so I'd get fired. You're not taking any risk."

"All right. Well, this judge—a dear, kindly-looking old man with a heart of ice—kept on asking about the manner in which I was living, and how and where Rosabel would be brought up if he assigned her to me.

"That was awkward of his bloody lordship, because of course I was living with Eddie Sadler, which was what the divorce had all been about. And Eddie's a darling, and a rampant bull in bed, but his reputation isn't of the finest, let's face it."

"So that's why you're here as Phoebe Sadler—married again."

"Not yet in the sight of the Registrar," Phoebe explained. "But we will be, provided I get my hands on this lovely money. That's one of Eddie's characteristics. He's really fond of money. He's quite anxious about it, and he came down here and put up at the Crown on Monday, so as he could come and see me next day and find out how I'd got on. You may have noticed him. We were taking tea together. Of course, Philip hanging himself makes quite a difference."

"How you'd got on about what?" asked Kate.

"The judge, in his wisdom, said we should go away and try to agree together which of us was to have custody of Rosabel, the other having reasonable access. Then we were to see him again, either to tell him we'd agreed or, if we hadn't, to get his decision."

She paused and absent-mindedly bit her lower lip. For the first time, Kate was sorry for her. It had not been, she understood, entirely a question of money.

"You and Mr. Antrobus were to meet here, hidden from all publicity, to discuss it," she said gently.

"That's right," Phoebe replied, hard again. "We had to decide which would have Rosabel, and what access would be reasonable for the other. Philip was not at all co-operative, either on those questions or on the really important one."

"Which was?"

"Money, of course. Eddie said I ought to be able to screw twenty thousand pounds out of him as the price of forgoing Rosabel. But Eddie had misjudged Philip. He said he felt pretty such that, if we couldn't agree, the judge would give Rosabel to him. I got an uneasy feeling that Philip had something cooking; he usually had, the bastard. But he said it would be better if we agreed, so if I wanted a little parting gift, he'd run to a thousand quid, and that was all. We had quite a ding-dong about it."

"Here, in this room," asked Kate, "at about eight o'clock on Monday evening?"

"That's right. Oh, of course, the walls are thin. How much did you hear?"

"Nothing," Kate assured her. "I heard him when he was out on the balcony, saying he wasn't going to buy it. Then he went into the room, and although I could make out a woman's voice raised in argument, I couldn't hear any of the words. The walls are not that thin."

"Not that it matters," said Phoebe. "I don't give a damn, whatever you heard. What in fact he said was that he was pretty desperate about the way his finances were going, and there just wasn't any money to spare for me—not my kind of money, anyway.

"So I asked him, what about Rosabel then? He said she'd be all right, if he got custody. So long as he was alive, he'd be perfectly able to keep her in comfort. When he died, there was the insurance policy on his life he had taken out in her favour. There were certain provisions about her not getting the capital until she was twenty-one, but she'd get the income straight away. His solicitors would be Rosabel's trustees.

"But if he didn't get custody, he said, he would cash in

the life policy at its surrender value and forget he ever had a child."

"Nobody could do that."

"Philip probably could. But what puzzles me is why he argued about it at all, if he were going to kill himself that night. He couldn't have been intending to when he was talking to me; that wouldn't make sense. He must have acted on impulse later. He had already drunk a lot of scotch. He wasn't fuddled, but if he went on drinking . . ."

"He did," said Kate.

"That must be it. Anyway, he's dead. The dead don't matter—but their life policies do. I was with him when he took out that life insurance. He did it directly Rosabel was born, nearly four years ago. He insured his life, in her favour, for three hundred thousand pounds. That's what I want to see the policy for—to find out if there's a suicide clause in it."

"You mean, if he committed suicide, the policy would be void? That clause is usually only for the first three years that the policy runs."

"Exactly. That's what I want to check."

She laid the document on the table, pushing other papers on to the floor. She turned the pages one by one, scanning the clauses.

Kate, looking over her shoulder, spotted the suicide clause. "There you are," she said, putting her finger on it.

They read it together and Phoebe grunted with relief. The exclusion was for only the first three years of the policy.

"So Rosabel gets the money," she murmured. "Eddie will be so pleased."

CHAPTER 10

HENRY PHONED Kate while she was still in bed on Thursday morning, sipping her boiled water; she had already eaten her half-grapefruit. Scattered on the bed were the contents of the thick envelope Butch had sent her—photostats of sample Press clippings of Philip Antrobus and the girls he had been most photographed with over the years; a precis of gossip-column paragraphs about him and Phoebe, Janet Dimpsey and Bella; a list of companies in the Antrobus Enterprises empire, with brief notes on what each did, to which Butch had added copies of Press stories about a few of them.

"I'm starting to come round to your opinion, Kate," Henry told her.

"That's sensible of you, darling. Any particular reason?"

"Yes. But not on the phone. I'll come to Gorsedene."

"Not before twelve o'clock," she instructed. "My treatments, remember? Come to my room. If we're going to talk about all that, it had better be in private. I've a couple of revelations for you, too."

The morning's treatments went to the usual pattern. The female heads in the steam bath-house were nodding and gossiping as vigorously as ever. Bella, in the next cabinet, was cheerful and amusing. Norah, the masseuse, however, was still glum.

When she had Kate on the table and was kneading the base of her spine, she told her that the tension in her back had eased almost completely. She should aim to get deep massage once in every three months, and she'd have no more back trouble; otherwise, it could lead to arthritis.

"Thanks," said Kate. "I'll remember that."

When she was shifted on to her side, and Norah was working on her legs, Kate asked, "Have you heard any more about Gorsedene's future?"

Norah looked miserable. "Mr. Dimpsey has let it be known to the staff that it's all very uncertain. There's a rumour going round that he intends to pack it in, and go abroad. We all know he's had several tempting offers in the past to start a health farm in America. He won't suffer. He's the best man in the world at his job. But what about us staff? Now lie on your other side, please, Mrs. Theobald."

When she had turned, Kate said: "You'd have no difficulty getting another job."

"Probably not. But where would I find anything to compare with Gorsedene?"

On the way back to her room Kate met Janet Dimpsey on the first-floor landing, arranging a magnificent bowl of roses for a table at the head of the first flight of stairs.

"Are you better?" asked Kate. "I was so sorry to hear of your migraine."

"Yes, thank you, Mrs. Theobald."

She did not look as though she had completely recovered, Kate thought. She had made up her face carefully, but the cosmetics could not hide the shadows under her eyes.

"It's a wretched thing, migraine," Kate said. "My mother suffers from it. Agony while the attack lasts."

Janet Dimpsey agreed. "I used to get attacks more frequently when I was younger. But Pelham put me on a herbal treatment that really worked pretty well, on the whole. I get attacks now only when I'm worried." She gave a nervous laugh. "We've had plenty to worry us this week. The migraine I had on Tuesday was an absolute beast. I could scarcely bear to open my eyes. I had to lie all day in a darkened room. It was good of you to help Pelham out with those newspaper reporters. Anything like that terrifies him, and I usually handle it."

"It was nothing," said Kate. "By the way, I hear your husband is thinking of resigning from Gorsedene and perhaps going to America."

"We've often talked of it. He could make much more money out there, and it would be better for Christopher. But while Philip was alive we felt a certain tie of loyalty. We were such old friends, and he had been very good to Pelham, starting him off here. But now this awful thing has happened . . ."

She was on the edge of tears.

Kate touched her shoulder sympathetically. "I know. Don't distress yourself."

Janet looked at her for a moment, her face pale, her hand nervously touching her lips. Then she turned abruptly and hastened away through a service door, unable to control her weeping.

2

"She seems very distressed," said a voice behind Kate.

She turned and saw Michael, who had come along the thick-carpeted corridor.

"With good reason," she replied. "Philip Antrobus was an old friend and his death has knocked her badly. On top of that, he was arranging for her husband to take over Gorsedene. Now that must fall through. The place will certainly change hands and may be shut down."

"That'd be a pity."

"It would be worse than a pity for the Dimpseys. The wretched woman loses her home, a sure future, and her husband's position. They may emigrate to America. To cap everything, she's a migraine subject. All day Tuesday, prostrate with the shock, she lay in agony in a darkened room."

Michael shook his head sympathetically.

"But if they're going to the States," he said, "I might be able to help. Dimpsey would surely need capital to start up, and off the cuff I could name a half-dozen rich men in Washington who'd be delighted to invest in an American Gorsedene. I'll mention it to Dimpsey. I'm just going along to see him. Mary and I are planning to fly back to the States on Saturday."

Kate regarded him thoughtfully. "What about Senator

Galahad? What if Antrobus really had proof of his corruption?"

Michael looked uneasy. "I can sort that out when I get back to Washington. And I'll lay odds it's a phoney. I know that senator so well. What's for sure is that, whatever evidence Antrobus had, or had cooked up, I won't ever see it."

"Why not? He may not have been the only man in his business organization to know of it. They may still try to put pressure on you by producing the evidence to you."

"I doubt it," said Michael. "An old friend of mine, an Englishman who was at Harvard on a bursary in my year, is now a partner in one of your biggest law firms. I called him this morning and told him, without giving any details, that the Antrobus interests might try to get my support in their fight over the defence contract, and what did he advise? He said to forget it. There's little doubt, he said, that a liquidator will be put into the Antrobus group. Your stock market has already halted any further dealing in its shares. The American defence contract probably lapses anyway, in those circumstances."

Kate wondered whether she should jump him now with the fact that she knew of *The Vice Kings*, and the truth about the blackmail. Even if the commercial reason for it no longer existed, she reasoned to herself, there was the ordinary kind of blackmail, for money. There were probably other copies of the typescript, and the man most likely to make use of them was almost certainly privy to what Antrobus was doing—John Sherwood.

Then she gaped in astonishment. A door farther along the corridor opened abruptly and a man came striding angrily out, scowling. John Sherwood.

He was followed by Pelham Dimpsey. It was the door to the director's consulting-rooms.

Dimpsey was protesting apologetically that there was nothing he could do about it. The matter was out of his hands.

"Go to hell," replied Sherwood curtly.

He glared at Kate and Michael, but said nothing as he stepped past them and down the stairs. Pelham Dimpsey followed slowly, then halted at the head of the stairs, with a distressed look at the retreating figure of John Sherwood.

"Is there any way I can be of help, Mr. Dimpsey?" asked Michael.

"No way, I'm afraid. Mr. Sherwood wants to collect the business papers from Philip's room. Very naturally, of course. Mr. Sherwood is trying to keep Philip's enterprises in motion, and there's no doubt that he needs those business papers."

Kate saw the shadow of dismay that crossed Michael's eyes.

"But you say that he can't have them, Mr. Dimpsey?" she asked.

Pelham Dimpsey turned towards her. "Sergeant Grey has informed me that the room must remain locked until after the inquest tomorrow, and nothing must be disturbed there, and nobody admitted."

"Isn't that a little officious of the sergeant?"

"It is not Sergeant Grey's doing," Dimpsey assured her. "He tells me he has received orders from his superiors—originally, he says, from the Chief Constable himself. It seems that a Scotland Yard officer is coming here and has applied for a magistrate's order giving him access to those documents. Sergeant Grey gave me explicit instructions this morning, from the Chief Constable, not to allow anybody into that room. So, of course, I must obey. What it's all about, Sergeant Grey says he simply does not know. He himself is genuinely puzzled by it."

"Understandably," Kate agreed.

3

Henry was in the hall, saw Kate, and she called to him to come to her room.

He had to wait while she dressed before she would listen to the news he said he had for her.

"Are you admiring my trim figure?" she asked.

"Rapturously."

"Well, don't get any immediate ideas, darling. I haven't the strength even to think of it."

She zipped up her dress and sat facing him. "Now then, you think I may be right. Why?"

He told her of the policeman at the Crown the previous evening and the theft of Pugh's valise during the night.

"And what does your legal mind make of all that?"

"Grant that it was murder and not suicide," he said. "There are immense difficulties in the way of that, but suppose it for the present.

"Charles Pugh, on the death of his mother—as most only sons are particularly tied to a widowed mother—suddenly discovers that the man whom he had always thought his benefactor was the man who had driven his father to death. I am also assuming, by the way, that Leonard Pugh, the father, in fact shot himself and was not shot by somebody else. If we're going to start postulating murder, there was a hell of a strong motive at that time for the murder of Leonard Pugh by Antrobus, Sherwood, or either of the two others who were in the syndicate and involved in the fraud, but of whom we otherwise know nothing."

"Like all converts," remarked Kate, "you're strong on your new beliefs. Go on."

"It must have been on Sunday night or Monday morning that Charles Pugh found his father's papers and realized what they meant."

"Because he flew Antrobus here on Sunday afternoon without any fuss or protest? Yes, I see that. Go on."

"Sherwood has to come back here on Monday evening, because of the Stock Exchange business. By the way, Kate, I've been on to Peter Lane this morning, and I'm glad to say the market is steadying. He thinks they've averted the danger of a general collapse. But there's not much doubt that Antrobus Enterprises really is bust. Sherwood didn't have to murder Antrobus to make a financial killing—if you see what I mean. All he had to do was to tell the syndicate to get cracking, because he would have known the extent of the company's troubles, and when they were likely to come to light. It was a quite normal, if extremely dirty bear raid."

"Don't side-track," ordered Kate. "I want to know about Charles Pugh."

"All right. But let me add one more thing about Sherwood and his Stock Exchange coup. I guess it may well have been that original fraud that he feared would come to light if Antrobus Enterprises were probed by a liquidator. So it's quite likely that, knowing the liquidation was imminent, he set off the bear operation to make himself enough to bolt for Brazil or some other non-extradition country."

"All right," said Kate impatiently. "But Charles Pugh?"

"He flies here on Monday afternoon with those damning notes from his father in his valise. He storms into Antrobus's room in a raging temper, throws up his job and tells them why—Sherwood was there, too, wasn't he?"

"I think so."

"We don't know what went on at that interview, but I can guess. Pugh told them he was taking the notes to the police."

"Then why didn't he do just that?" asked Kate.

"Perhaps Antrobus simply laughed at the threat, and said the trail had been covered long ago. If that is what Antrobus told him, he was bluffing. Stoddart, the Scotland Yard man who now has the notes, reckons they're just the evidence he has been looking for for three years.

"But Pugh would have believed Antrobus. So he thought there was no revenge by going to the police. He went downstairs, collected his valise from the porter, and got into the taxi. Before he reached the station he decided upon another kind of revenge. He must have been half crazy with rage by then. So he took a room at the Crown and, later in the evening, went quietly back to Antrobus's room—and Antrobus would have admitted him. He then murdered the man by stringing him up to that pipe by the cord of his dressing-gown.

"How? That's the great difficulty. But we'll come back to that. Pugh then slipped away as quietly as he had come."

"Why didn't he go back to the Crown?" asked Kate.

"Lost his nerve, I suppose. Can you imagine the state of mind of an ordinary, respectable young man who had killed a man in a rage. He wouldn't be capable of thinking rationally. He probably bolted through the woods, thumbed a lift to London or something . . ."

"He didn't return to his house in London," Kate pointed out. "It was broken into that night, and he wasn't there."

"Maybe he's still on the run, desperate to know what to do."

"Yesterday morning," mused Kate, "he realized he'd have to get his valise back from the Crown. So it was he who broke in last night and took it?"

"It could be," Henry agreed. "I hadn't thought of that."

Kate said, "Henry, there's still the question I raised yesterday, which you rather pooh-poohed. The landlord of the Crown got telephoned instructions to send the valise and Pugh's bill to the Antrobus office in London. How did anyone in the office know the bag was there?"

Henry considered. "Sherwood. That must be the answer. He was as deeply implicated in those notes as Antrobus, and must have been grimly anxious to get hold of them. Maybe one of the thugs on his payroll broke into Pugh's house on Tuesday night. It's well known that he has a dirty-tricks department."

"But how did he know the bag was at the Crown?"

"If it was one of Sherwood's boys who burgled Pugh's house, he might have known Pugh wasn't there, and so tried locally on spec., and phoned the Crown. Or maybe Sergeant Grey told him. He must have known about the bag left behind. I don't know for sure, but Sherwood could have found out one way or another. And then, not certain that Toomey would send it to the Antrobus office, or perhaps wondering if it might be taken by the police, he sent one of his thugs into the Crown last night to collect it, to make sure. I don't think your question is an absolute block, Kate. What bothers me much more is, how did Pugh do it—how did he overcome Antrobus and hang him to that pipe?"

Henry walked into her bathroom, staring at the pipe. Kate followed him.

"How could a man loop another man's dressing-gown

cord around his neck, and string him up to that pipe? It's not possible."

"Even if Antrobus were in a daze? He'd got through a lot of whisky."

"He'd have to be in a stupor to let that happen to him," Henry answered. "Even if he had drunk himself into a coma, Pugh would have had to be immensely strong to haul him up to that pipe."

"He looked a burly young man. Rather dishy, as a matter of fact."

"I suppose two men could have done it. But Pugh couldn't have had a second man with him." Henry shook his head. "It's just not feasible, Kate. I've constructed a lovely theory, but it doesn't work. Faced with the collapse of his fortune, and the threat of going to gaol for fraud, Philip Antrobus hanged himself. That's that."

"Then why didn't Charles Pugh go back to the Crown for his bag?" asked Kate.

"God knows."

4

They returned from the bathroom into Kate's room. She rested on the bed and Henry took a chair by the window.

"I've discovered a little of what happened in Antrobus's room on Monday evening," she said. "I now know who the woman is he was arguing with at about eight o'clock."

She told of her encounter with Phoebe Sadler.

"There's a motive for you, wouldn't you say?" she concluded.

"Fascinating," Henry agreed. "But there's no point in discovering a motive for a crime she couldn't have committed. I doubt if a man could have hanged Antrobus from that pipe in those circumstances. Certainly no woman could. Physically impossible."

"Eddie was in the neighbourhood that evening."

"Eddie?"

"Eddie Sadler. I told you—the co-respondent in the divorce who will marry her, she says, if she can get her hands on enough of Antrobus's money. Eddie thought she ought to shake him down for twenty thousand pounds for surrendering the child to him. In the event, he offered her one thousand pounds. And he made it clear that he wouldn't give her any more. But Rosabel would be all right, if he had custody. And when he died, she would get his life insurance. Phoebe happened to know that his life was insured for three hundred thousand pounds. So . . ."

"So she goes back to her room and phones Eddie to come round from the Crown," Henry pursued thoughtfully. "They talk it over. If Antrobus dies, she will get custody of the child. There's nobody else. So she will get the income from three hundred thousand pounds, and probably be able to fiddle quite a lot of the capital. If Antrobus dies . . ."

"We don't know anything about Eddie," said Kate, "except that he sounds unscrupulous—and he's a bull in bed. So Eddie asks her if there is a suicide clause in that life policy. She tells him she thinks so, but she's not sure He reckons it's a good bet that it would be the usual clause, operative only for the first three years of the policy. Phoebe assures him that that would be all right, because the policy was taken out at Rosabel's birth, and the child is well past her third birthday.

"But then she's puzzled. She asks Eddie how that helps, since Philip isn't going to kill himself anyway. Eddie smiles, and remarks that he might, because judging by the stock market that afternoon, Philip was bust. So he might kill himself that very night.

"Then Eddie smiles again and murmurs that perhaps they could give him a little assistance in the matter."

Keeping up the game, Henry asked, "How does Phoebe take it, when she realizes what Eddie is suggesting?"

"Coolly, I think," said Kate. "She's a hard bitch—and I guess she craves Eddie passionately. She's hooked sexually. What's more, she hates Philip. She made that quite plain. The only touch of genuine emotion she displayed was, for a moment, about wanting the child."

"This is all nonsense, of course," Henry told her, smiling. "There's not even a glimpse of evidence."

"Darling, don't be so legalistic. Even if it's a fanciful

story, let's try to finish it. Phoebe and Eddie realize that there'll never be another time when Philip Antrobus's suicide would seem so plausible."

" 'If it were done when 'tis done,' quoted Henry, 'then 'twere well it were done quickly.' Did Lady Macbeth play her part, do you think?"

"Possibly," declared Kate excitedly. "It overcomes the objection you keep on raising. A man could not have hanged Antrobus unaided, but with a little help . . . "

"She takes Eddie along to Antrobus's room," Henry continued. "They want to talk about Rosabel. Antrobus lets them in. He has been drinking ever since Sherwood came down with details of the stock-market crash. The chap has had one hell of an evening, you know. Young Pugh has threatened to expose him to criminal prosecution. His business is collapsing. His ex-wife has tried to extort a fortune out of him. Not surprising that he punished that bottle of scotch.

"So he's muzzy. The woman distracts him while the man loops the cord of his dressing-gown round his neck, pulling it tight to stop him yelling. The man tugs him into the bathroom. She jumps on the stool to slip the end of the cord over that pipe. Is she tall enough?"

"Yes, I think so."

"The man seizes the end of the cord and hauls Antrobus clear of the ground. He hangs on grimly to the cord until the victim is dead, then scrambles up on the stool to knot the end round the pipe. To make it feasible, it remains only to kick the stool over against the wall . . . "

"The thud I heard!" exclaimed Kate. "It was a chair overturning that made the thud I heard today. It could have been the stool that made the thud on Monday night. Do you believe any of this, Henry?"

He grinned cheerfully. "Not a word of it, darling. An exercise in imagination, that's all. No matter how muzzy Antrobus was, do you find it even faintly credible that he could have been murdered like that without a struggle. And there was no struggle. If you could hear the thud of a stool being kicked over, you would certainly have heard a fight."

Kate had sadly to agree. "And yet," she murmured, "there is the three hundred thousand pound insurance policy. It's a wonderful motive."

"Isn't it about time for your lunch?" asked Henry pleasantly. "If I don't leave now, I'll be late for mine. Just a cold buffet—ham and tongue or veal-and-ham pie, with a mixed salad and boiled potatoes. Treacle tart to follow. I asked Mrs. Toomey before I came, because I felt sure you'd like to know."

"Go," she implored weakly. "Don't say any more. Just go."

5

When he reached the Crown, he went into the saloon bar for a quick pint.

"I called in Sergeant Grey about the theft of Mr. Pugh's bag," Jerry Toomey told him as he drew the beer. "And I phoned that office in London where I was to send it."

"What did they say?"

"I gave the message to a girl on the line. She said she'd pass it on to Mr. Sherwood."

"And the sergeant?"

"He reckoned it was a break-in all right."

Henry laughed. "Good for the sergeant! A neat deduction from a window jemmied open."

"Footprints in the flowerbed outside, too," said Toomey. "Sergeant Grey measured them, and said he'd get his inspector to send round a fingerprint man, to see what he could find in my office. He hasn't come yet."

"The law moves slowly, but surely," Henry promised as he finished his pint. "I must go and clean up, ready for Mrs. Toomey's excellent veal-and-ham pie."

"She do make a good one. Quite well-known for her pies Lucy is, round these parts."

Henry climbed the stairs and noticed that the door to his room was ajar; nobody bothered about room keys at the Crown. The cleaner must have left it open.

Then he halted and stared into the room with bewilderment.

His briefs and all his notes were strewn around the floor. One of his law books had been torn apart. All his clothes had been pulled from drawers and hanging cupboard and scattered around.

"What the hell . . . !" he exclaimed, stepping into the room.

The blow that knocked him out struck the back of his head. He fell across the bed.

CHAPTER 11

AFTER HENRY left her, Kate picked up the bundle which Butch had sent and began to meander through it.

First she looked at the clippings about the women. Butch had sent separate batches linking Philip Antrobus with Phoebe before she married him, with Janet Lockwood (which was Janet Dimpsey's maiden name), and with Bella.

The batch about Bella was thicker than Kate had expected. Bella had had much more to do with the man than she had pretended.

Kate reached for the telephone and asked for her half-grapefruit and jug of boiled water—"Lemon flavour, please"—to be sent to her room. The clippings needed her immediate attention.

The significance of those about Bella was that she had been associated with Antrobus over a period of nearly two years. There were pictures of them at parties, at a film première, at a race meeting; gossip paragraphs using the stock euphemisms for announcing that she was his mistress. The paragraphs became most mischievous about four years ago, which was when he married Phoebe (who must, Kate realized, have been five or six months pregnant with Rosabel at the time of the ceremony; she looked quickly at the Phoebe clippings; there were no photographs of the wedding, but only half-column head-and-shoulders blocks that could have been made at any time).

The other significant thing was that the association between Antrobus and Bella seemed to have continued for about six months after he married Phoebe, and then stopped abruptly. After that, no more about Bella. Was that the date of the motor-cruiser party? Kate wondered.

Whether or not, why had Bella lied to her about how little she had known Philip Antrobus? It seemed such a pointless lie.

She picked up the Phoebe clippings. Those dated before her marriage usually called her a top model, or sometimes a starlet; she had had a small part in a movie of which Kate had never heard.

One clipping gave a brief biography. She was daughter of a major-general—socialite, as one columnist put it. She had been to that school in Kent, was too young to have been presented, but was still written of as a débutante. She had fluttered around in Chelsea during the late 'sixties, being seen at all the required parties with several of the most notably dissolute young men.

From the earlier photographs she had clearly been a considerable beauty.

The longest article after her marriage was a women's-page feature about the way she had decorated Antrobus's Chelsea house; had had it more or less gutted, then remade with every possible extravagance. But after that the clippings diminished noticeably, as though, having married her, Antrobus had continued his bachelor-style life, paying her less and less heed. Even Rosabel's birth was only tangentially mentioned; the inevitable uneasiness, Kate gathered, about dates.

Most of the clippings about Janet Lockwood (later Janet Dimpsey) were earlier than those of the two other women. She appeared as Antrobus's girl-friend almost from the time when newspapers started writing about him at all. As her husband had told Kate, it was she who had introduced him to Antrobus.

In those early photographs, around the mid-'sixties, she looked wonderfully young, and quite enticing. She had that air of fresh, innocent sexuality that television ads try to capture for their soft-drinks, package-holidays or hair-fixing-lotion promotions; naivety combined with experience, diffidence with eagerness. As the years went by, the innocence faded from her expression, but the loveliness remained. By the time the Bella and Phoebe clippings started, Janet's practically finished. Since then there were only three or four references to her, all in connection with Gorsedene, her husband, and Antrobus's interest in the place.

Kate laid the clippings aside and picked up a batch of papers that Butch had sent, the list of companies in the Antrobus empire, with brief notes on what each did.

It was an impressive list, and well diversified. There were thirty-five companies ranging from a merchant bank to a small chain of grocery shops in the Midlands, from property developers and builders to an investment company in the Channel Islands, a tea importer with plantations in Sri Lanka and India, a mail-order business, a near-pornography publishing house, a textile wholesaler, a timber importer, a stone quarry, a coastal shipping-freight line, a plant-hire outfit, an advanced electronics engineering concern, a number of financial, insurance and trading houses which were merely confusing to Kate, the recording company of which Bella had spoken, confectionery manufacturers, and several small enterprises of which Gorsedene, the health farm, was one. It was linked, Kate saw, with a chain of health-food stores in big-city suburbs, and she guessed that Pelham Dimpsey was the technical expert for those, as well as director of Gorsedene.

A note from Butch told her that by far the most important component of Antrobus Enterprises was the firm making advanced electronic equipment. Much of it was highly-classified defence stuff, and it was in an American defence contract by this company that Antrobus had been most deeply, and possibly disastrously committed. If that went wrong, Antrobus Enterprises would probably founder; and it threatened to go wrong because of a complex financial arrangement which had taken insufficient precautions against escalating costs in the then unforeseen period of rapid inflation. Antrobus had been trying to get those financial clauses modified to fit the realities of present and likely future costs. He had a fair amount of sympathetic backing in Washington, but a few inflexible and overwhelmingly powerful opponents.

To several of the bare outlines of other companies in the list Butch had added similar notes, or a couple of newspaper clippings, chiefly from the financial columns.

There had been a police prosecution of the publishing

house over one book, which had been ordered to be destroyed. One of the insurance companies was in severe trouble because it had over-sold cut-price motor insurance and could not meet ever-rising costs of repair claims. A property company had come in for a share of public criticism of office blocks built and left untenanted while rent levels soared; and had found itself with potential white elephants when rent levels dropped.

The tea importers were in trouble on their plantations because of alleged maltreatment of the workers. To notes on this company Butch had pinned copy from a Reuters man in Calcutta which, he had scribbled on it, had not been used, so far as he knew, in any British newspaper.

It was a depth report on what had nearly been violent revolt in Assam. This centred on a number of tea plantations, of which those owned by the Antrobus company were the largest and most vilified. There had been riots on the plantations themselves, attacks on company-owned stores and administrative buildings, and mob violence in a small town lying in the midst of the plantations. Four people had been killed—one of them a policeman—and upwards of eighty injured. Large numbers of police had been sent in to quell the rioters.

The cause of the troubles was conditions of the plantation workers. They were paid starvation wages, their housing was primitive and there was virtually no medical service, though disease was rife. In slack times of the year, the workers—men as well as women—were laid off without wages. There were the usual tales of families selling their children for a few bags of rice.

Kate was suddenly acutely aware that she was reading this in a health farm where overfed men and women were paying £100 a week to be force-starved. She felt a little sick.

The Reuters man had toured the area in Assam and vouched for the truth of most of the allegations. The conditions had been seized upon, he wrote, by a small group of Calcutta intellectuals who, together with a few activists, had started and kept up the violence. The reporter had interviewed one of the leaders of the group, son of a local family who had got himself to university with the help of missionaries. He had insisted that they were not Marxists or Maoists. There was no international subversion for which they were making a front. They were violent because no other course seemed practical. About this, however, the reporter was doubtful; he suspected Maoism.

The insurgents had been beaten back by the lathis of police. But they were only temporarily checked, the leader of the group said. The struggle would not end until the tea planters gave in. They could not cease the struggle, he said, while such terrible conditions existed. He instanced his own family. His mother and one sister had died of virtual starvation. His father was a physical wreck. And his family was by no means the worst sufferer.

They had learned, the group leader said, that they could not prevail against the strength of the police. But, he added grimly, there were other ways.

The group leader had made no attempt to withhold his name. It was Charan Lal.

Kate stared at that last sentence in astonishment. Lal, she knew, was a common enough name in India. She did not know whether Charan was also.

It could, of course, be coincidence. The man she must talk to was Michael Neal.

She put the report in her handbag and went to look for him.

As she stepped out into the thickly-carpeted corridor, she saw that the door of Antrobus's room was slowly opening.

Kate stopped in silence, held her breath, waited.

The door opened cautiously. A head emerged nervously to see if the corridor was clear.

It was Mary Neal.

2

The woman started, then laughed nervously. "Are you always there?"

"Chance," said Kate, "or Providence. I know what you were looking for, and that you didn't find it."

Mary Neal stared at her. "You know?"

"Come into my room," suggested Kate. "We ought to talk."

Mary hesitated, but then followed her in. "How do you know that I didn't find it?"

"Because I have it."

Mary almost collapsed into a chair, drooping her head into her hands, murmuring, "Thank God. Thank God."

"It doesn't necessarily solve anything," said Kate quietly. "Hadn't you better tell me?"

The other was trying to control herself, gradually calming.

"I had to find it," she began. "Michael is almost desperate, so tense. It could lead to a breakdown. And it was my fault. I put in there."

Kate was puzzled: "We are talking of the same thing, aren't we? The typescript of a dirty book and photostats of some cheap magazine articles?"

"Yes, of course."

"Then you say you put them there . . . ?"

"Michael went to Mr. Antrobus's room that evening, to plead with him. You know what was happening?"

"I can guess," said Kate. "Antrobus was trying to compel Michael to make, in his column, false accusations of corruption against a senator who was blocking Antrobus's plans in Washington."

"That's it—nearly so, anyhow."

"The threat being to publish that book, which would link you with vice rackets?"

"It is untrue," Mary protested tearfully. "But if it were published, how would it not be believed?"

"You were the girl in the picture?"

Mary nodded forlornly. "I was eighteen, not long out of school. I came to New York and got a job on the florist counter of a store. That was where Victor saw me. He was charming. I know now of his wickedness, but I did not know then. And I was young, and joyful at being in the great city, and he was charming . . ."

"You had no idea what he was doing?"

"Not until he wantd to set me up in an apartment for other men to visit. Then I ran. I was terrified, but I ran. I ran first to Detroit, where I had a cousin to help me.

Not long after that Victor was first arrested and charged. My cousin knew nothing of my association with him. I dared not tell her.

"Then one day I saw one of Victor's men, and I thought he had seen me. So I ran again. I ran to Chicago, and got work helping in a children's charity.

"A little later there was a charities congress in Washington, and I went as my boss's aide. That was where I met Michael. We went out a couple of times. He is a wonderful person. Then, when he suddenly arrived in Chicago, I knew he was in earnest.

"I told him all about Victor Zucconi. He said it was of no consequence. If he started to tell me all the murkier stories of his own life, he said, he would be talking for a year.

"We went on vacation in Canada, and married very quietly in a small town. Michael had to fly to Paris for an international meeting, and he took me. After that, it seemed quite natural for him to return to Washington with a bride. We have been so happy, until . . ."

"Antrobus?"

"He came to Washington on business about his contract, and while he was there he tried to persuade Michael to write these foul things. Michael refused, of course. Then Mr. Antrobus showed him that photograph and those articles. There was a book, he said, which was more explicit. He would publish that book, unless Michael chose to buy the copyright—and he knew the price.

"Mr. Antrobus was returning to England next day. He said Michael was to come as his guest to Gorsedene, and should see the book. We had to come.

"On Monday Mr. Antrobus gave him copies of several pages of the book. They were horrible. They were false as hell, but who would believe that when they knew I was once, for a short time, Victor Zucconi's girl?"

"Was Michael going to give in?"

"I feared he would. If he did, it would destroy him. If he had to print those lies in his column, he said, he would. But then he would stop writing. He would leave journalism. He is the only truly honest person I have ever met."

"There aren't many," Kate agreed, mock ruefully, trying to assess the situation.

"I thought of killing myself," whispered Mary. "I had some drugs. I really thought of that, as the best way. Michael guessed, and took the bottle of tablets from my drawer. Then he went to Mr. Antrobus's room to plead with him not to go on with it."

"And then?" asked Kate, beginning to understand.

"He came back to our room very soon. He brought the book manuscript and the articles with him. He had found the room empty, he said, and had picked them up and taken them.

"I begged him to return them. It would merely make Mr. Antrobus angry, and it was pointless because there would be other copies of the manuscript. But Michael refused to return them. He was in an excited state. He went into the bathroom to plunge his face into cold water.

"On impulse, I picked up the papers and went to Mr. Antrobus's room. The door was still open. I went in. Nobody was there. I dropped the book and the articles on the table and hurried out.

"Michael had guessed where I had gone, and followed. As I came out, he tried to push past me to get the things back again. That was when you interrupted us."

"You thought there was no point in taking the typescript, but Michael thought there was. Why?"

After a long hesitation Mary said, in a low voice, "I did not know that Mr. Antrobus was already dead."

"And Michael did?"

"I have not asked him."

"Then we should ask him now," decided Kate. "Where is he?"

"In our room."

Kate asked the switchboard for a connection to Mr. Neal's room, then handed the phone to Mary.

"I am in Mrs. Theobald's room, Michael. She knows. And she has—those things. Will you come, please?"

"By the way," asked Kate while they waited, "how did you get into Antrobus's room just now? It was kept locked by police orders."

"Charan Lal gave me the pass key. I said Michael wanted it. Charan would do anything for Michael."

3

He was excited when he came in.

"You have that typescript? My dear Kate . . ."

"Not so fast. I want to know a little more first."

"He was trying to blackmail me."

"Yes," said Mary, "she knows all that."

"It was a carefully planned plot, Kate. Antrobus was quite frank about it. He told me he had decided that the most effective, perhaps the only way of forcing a certain senator to get out of his path and allow him to save his contract and his whole financial standing, was to have me make scurrilous accusations in my column. The only place, he said quite blatantly, where there had never been a lie, so any lie would be believed. After the first couple of paragraphs, he explained, there would be a quiet approach to the senator, telling him exactly how he could prevent many more."

"You told him to go to hell?"

"Of course. Then Antrobus told me what he proposed. He had a dirty-book publishing house in London, from which he had sent his shrewdest editor to Washington, to search files of the pulp rags. Every eminent American, he declared, is bound to have been libelled in the pulps at some time, either about himself, or his family.

"The editor had Mary's maiden name, and he found it in an obscure list of Victor Zucconi's girl-friends; just the name, nothing more. So then he concentrated on Zucconi, and spotted that photograph in a series of pulp articles by a drunken old hack named Karasak.

"The editor found Karasak and offered him a considerable sum to work the articles up into a book, *The Vice Kings*. No need to bother about further research, he told him, but just to use his imagination, particularly about Mary Pastorelli.

"It was a death sentence for Heinz Karasak, of course. Perhaps Antrobus counted on that, to get an awkward witness out of the way. With that money, he was in an alcoholics hospital inside a couple of months. He insisted on discharging himself, and a few weeks later he was dead. Is there anything else you want to know?"

Kate nodded. She asked him why he had thought there would be any point in taking the typescript, since Antrobus must surely have had at least one other copy.

"I was overwrought, not thinking straight," said Michael awkwardly.

"The odd thing is," she pursued, "that you turned out to be right. It was worth taking the typescript, because Philip Antrobus is dead. Did you know he was already dead?"

Michael Neal looked sadly at her. "I was afraid you would guess that. Yes, I knew. When I went along to his room to plead with him, I found the door ajar and the room empty. But the bathroom door was half open, and I could see him swinging there. So I found the typescript and took it.

"There were still risks, of course. Probably there were other copies, and the editor at the publishing house would know their significance."

"Of course he would," said Kate.

"But that can be coped with. As a matter of fact, that is already arranged. I explained more frankly to my old college friend, the English lawyer, than I told you I had. I did give him the details, and he came up with the solution. When a liquidator is put in at Antrobus Enterprises, my friend will make a discreet proxy bid for the copyrights owned by the publishing house. He reckons the liquidator will be glad to get in any cash he can, and I'll probably buy the copyrights for a thousand pounds or so. If that editor tries blackmail, my lawyer will know how to deal with him." Michael chuckled. "And he said that, when I had destroyed the Karasak book, I might sell off the others to some other pornography house. There could even be a small profit in it for me."

Kate said, "My husband is sure that Philip Antrobus hanged himself."

"What else?"

"I wonder if he were murdered."

Michael gaped at her. "I'm struggling to find the word the English would use. Flabbergasted, I think. Kate, I'm flabbergasted."

"Now you, Michael," she continued, facing him, "had a real motive, and you were there. I suppose you didn't kill him?"

"If flabbergasted isn't an absolute," he answered, "I'm the absolute. I'm flabbergastedest. No, Kate dear, I didn't kill him. Maybe I had murder in my heart—who hasn't at some time or other? But no, Kate, I didn't kill him. He was already hanged when I got to the room."

Kate smiled. "I said that only as shock tactics. But my idea isn't quite nonsense."

She handed him Butch's notes and the Reuters story on the Antrobus tea plantations.

Michael, puzzled, read it through. At the last paragraph, he gasped, "It must be coincidence."

"Must it?" asked Kate. "I found Charan Lal with two other Indians, a man and a girl, holding some sort of meeting in the woods on Monday afternoon."

"We've met the man," Michael told her. "Charan has an old jalopy. One afternoon, just before you arrived, he took us for a drive to show us the countryside. He stopped off at a cottage outside the little town, on the far side, to pick up some clothes. The other man was there. They're both students, and they've rented the place for the vacation. Lal is working here, as you know. The other man has a job in a gas-station. We didn't see any girl."

Kate took back the Reuters copy. "Charan is quoted here as saying that they couldn't beat the police, but there are other ways. There's one other way that fanatical terrorists have been using all over the world."

"Kidnapping?"

Kate nodded. "Why not?"

"Philip Antrobus himself," mused Michael. "It could have worked."

"Then perhaps something went wrong in the attempt, so they killed him by stringing him up to that pipe, to make it look like suicide."

"It's fantastic."

"You're friendly with Charan Lal, Michael. Talk to him

about Assam and the tea plantations. Then suddenly let him see that you know more than he thought you knew. Ask him what he meant to do. Say it jocularly—kidnap Philip Antrobus? See if you can jerk him into giving anything away."

"I'll try. But I doubt if he'll be easily jumped."

Mary asked anxiously, "The book and the articles?"

"I have them safe. Henry's the only other person who knows I have them. I won't let on to anyone else, and in the end I'll give them to you to destroy. But first I want to make sure there's nobody proposing to use some other copy to blackmail you."

"But I told you. Anybody like the editor in that publishing house can be coped with," said Michael.

"It could be somebody more sinister, somebody you'd never shake off."

Michael looked astonished. "But who?"

"I'm not sure. But there's one man—never mind who. If he should try it, there could be other ways of coping with him."

"Hadn't you better tell me?"

"Not until I'm sure."

CHAPTER 12

SHE MUST find Bella, Kate decided. She wanted an explanation.

Bella was not in the pool, or sunbathing round it. Phoebe was. She raised her hand lazily towards Kate, then let her head relax against the cushion on the back of her chair. One of the other patients, middle-aged, rather stout, probably a business man trying to fend off a thrombosis, was eyeing Phoebe speculatively, evidently thinking of a pick-up. Kate smiled. That stout old codger was wasting his time.

She walked past the gymnasium block and through the stable yard and the car park, to come round the far end of the main building and on to the front lawn. Bella was not among the patients grouped along the terrace, and it seemed highly unlikely that she had done anything so energetic as take herself for a walk.

Then Kate spotted her, stretched out on a long chair beneath the shade of an oak on the far side of the lawn, close to the river.

Kate picked up a deckchair and walked over.

Bella smiled sleepily. "Can't you stand the bleeding sun either? It brings me out in such freckles that even Number Nine won't cover them. And the cameras pick out every little pimple, let me tell you, without a miss."

When she had settled beside her, Kate remarked offhandedly that her news editor had sent her an interesting batch of newspaper clippings about Philip Antrobus. Bella asked why.

"I'll have to write something after the inquest tomorrow.

Everybody will be printing a lot of background material. Butch—that's my news editor—wants a piece from me about Antrobus's girl-friends."

By the length of the silence, she knew the point had been taken.

At last Bella, asked throatily, "He sent you a lot about the women Philip knew? Anything about me?"

"Quite a lot, Bella. I thought you said you had very little to do with him personally, until that party up the Thames. But I must have misunderstood you. There are heaps of pictures of you and him going places together, and gossip paragraphs of course, up to about six months after his marriage. I thought maybe I could interview you."

"Okay, so I was lying. What's it got to do with you?"

"Nothing," Kate admitted, "except that I do have this piece to write on the women Philip Antrobus knew. As a matter of interest, Bella, why did you lie? It seems so pointless."

"Because I didn't want to get into the publicity, that's why," said Bella thickly. "I've met up again lately with Reg, and he's still not wed, and I think there's a chance he might . . . But not if I come out in the middle of this mucky business."

"Why should you?"

"I knew the bastard all right. I wasn't going to bed with him, if that's what you're thinking. Anyway, only a few times. And he never tried none of that whipping lark on me. First I knew about that was on that party up the river. What I told you about that was true."

"About six months after he got married?"

"Yes, near enough. After that I never went out with him again. I was still working for his recording outfit, natch, because I'd got these contracts, see. But nothing personal any more."

"But that was about three years ago. Why should you be involved now?" Something dawned on Kate. "Bella, did you come here at this time specially to see him?"

Bella nodded sullenly. "I had to."

"Had to?"

"The bastard had got me by the short and curly. He wanted me to . . . Look, this ain't for your paper, is it?"

"I don't know until you tell me. What did he want you to do?"

"To go to some judge and give evidence against his ex-wife. He wanted to blacken her character, so that he'd get custody of the kid."

"What sort of evidence?"

Bella looked around at her. There was desperation in her eyes.

"I don't know what to do, and that's a fact. I'm in a bloody awful mess, Kate. If I'm not careful, I'll end up in prison."

"If it's any help," offered Kate, "you can tell me in confidence, not for publication."

Bella regarded her doubtfully. At last she said, "Really on the q.t.? S'elp you? He wanted me to say I'd supplied her with drugs, the hard stuff, and she's addicted."

"Is it true?"

"Shouldn't think she is. Not so far as I know. I never let her have any."

"You knew all along that she's here, calling herself Sadler?"

"Course I did, natch."

Kate waited. The explanation, she calculated, would be more likely to come if she kept silent. As it did. At last Bella began.

"The folks I mix with, pop groups and all that, singers, guitar players, tympany, there's a lot of drugging. I tried it meself, but never took to it. But some of the boys was desperate, and now and then I let 'em have a packet or two."

"Where did you get the drugs?"

"From John Sherwood. He was a supplier—probably still is. But I couldn't prove a thing against him. He took care of that. I was so stupid I didn't think anybody would ever know. I was stupid about something else, too. Payola. I dished out quite a bit, here and there, to get my discs played, and other numbers that Philip's outfit made."

"And the money came from Sherwood?"

"That's what I thought. Business promotion, on the quiet, he said. All I had to do was sign these few bits of paper. Monday, I found out where the dough really come from—and the hard stuff, too, though I couldn't prove that. Not Sherwood. He was only the carrier. Philip, of course, the shit."

Kate asked quietly, "How did you find that out on Monday? From Philip himself? Some time that evening? In his room?"

Bella was almost whimpering.

"Gawd, if I'd known he was going to kill himself . . ."

"Tell me."

"I was lying down that evening, watching the telly. He phoned me to come to his room."

"What time was that?"

"About a quarter after eight. Maybe a little later. I was watching Johnny on the telly. Shocking performance, all ham. As for that cow he had as guest star . . ."

"Then we can check the time," said Kate.

"Johnny started at eight. I'd watched about half his show—if you can call it a show. It'd be about quarter past all right."

"So you went to Philip's room."

"He was in that camp dressing-gown of his. He'd been drinking scotch, pretty hard. He offered me one, but I never touches it."

Remembering what she had lazily heard that evening, Kate asked, "Were you laughing at any time?"

"Laughing? What'd I got to laugh about?"

"That was when he told you you'd have to go before a judge and swear you'd been supplying Phoebe with heroin?"

"That's it. Or else there'd be a word or two slipped in the right quarter, and I'd have the fuzz on me tail, with drug-peddling charges, and payola, too, most like."

"What did you say?"

"What could I say? He'd got the proofs on me. I'd got to agree. So he said Sherwood would tell me where and when to show, and exactly what to say. If I done as I was told, I'd be in the clear and I'd hear no more about the other things. What the hell am I going to say if the police get around to me?"

"The police?" asked Kate, puzzled. "Why should they?"

"Because I was in his room, and it couldn't have been long before he done himself in."

"Have you told the police you were there? No? Then why should they ever know?"

"Mrs. Dimpsey could tell them."

Kate was startled. "Janet Dimpsey? She was there?"

"She come in. She'd some message from her husband. About the business they'd been discussing earlier, she said it was. So I took the hint, and scarpered—and was I glad to get away from the bastard! Do you reckon she will tell 'em?"

"I don't see why she should," Kate reassured her. "There's nothing much you could say that would help. You weren't the last person to see him alive."

"No. That'd be Mrs. Dimpsey."

2

It was time for the afternoon cup of tea. Kate would certainly not miss that. She was no longer hungry; that is, pangs no longer periodically gripped her, and she rarely now thought desperately of succulent dishes of food. Starvation was an odd experience, she mused. After so short a time—for this was only the fifth day—the body seemed to adapt itself to the absence of food, and not to care any more. Physically, of course, the body was affected. Kate was hugging to herself, like some gratifying secret, the exact figure at which she had dipped the scale when she was weighed that morning. She scarcely dared to dwell on it herself, and she had a curious fetish about telling anybody else, lest she tempt the gods. Certainly she would not tell Henry until the week was over and they were back home, and she felt strong enough to cope with the inevitable consequences of her new waistline.

Where, by the way, she wondered, was Henry? She had heard nothing from him all afternoon. Probably gorging himself into a stupor on that disgusting veal-and-ham pie and treacle tart, and was sleeping it off like a boa constrictor, the pig. Ah well, he'd surface eventually; certainly in time for dinner.

When she reached the terrace at the front of the house she saw the Neals at a table at the far end. She waved to them but did not join them. She wanted to sort things out in her own mind before discussing them with Henry when he next turned up.

Charan Lal arrived with the tea tray.

"With lemon, please, Charan."

He smiled politely and filled her cup.

There were two aspects on which she ought to concentrate. The trouble was, concentration seemed to be almost impossible at Gorsedene; however little starvation affected the body, it certainly stupefied the mind.

What would happen, she wondered, if one continued indefinitely? She remembered reading somewhere that there was an exact number of days before starvation led to death; forty-seven, she vaguely thought.

But, of course, it was not a question of simple starvation. One ate grapefruit. One drank water, and tea. Deprivation, but not complete starvation—the condition, of course, of the majority of mankind. Was this the reason, she wondered, for the backwardness of the Third World, this stupefaction of the mind and the spirit?

Damn! Her thoughts were wandering already.

The first thing to establish was everything she knew of what happened in Philip Antrobus's room on that Monday evening, reconstructing it from what she heard as she lay in bed, and from what she had since learned. Directly she tried, however, she felt she could not make any progress without pencil and paper; and she had no pencil and paper, and was far too lazy to go and fetch them. It would be easier to make that effort of memory when Henry was there to take control of her errant recollections.

The second point of concentration should be on what she had seen, or felt, or heard, that was wrong. She knew there was something. She had told Henry so on Monday night, when she first telephoned him. Ever since, she had now and then experienced uneasy moments of self-questioning.

There was something. Of that she was sure. She had a

feeling that it was something she had seen, which had registered in her subconscious as wrong. She giggled slightly to herself. Subconscious! It was about the only state of conscious she had in this place.

Something she had seen. What had she seen that was wrong? Wrong in what way? What sort of wrong?

She sighed, gave it up, finished her tea and, with a distant wave to the Neals, went up to her room to rest until "cocktail hour."

In fact she fell asleep and it was past seven in the evening when she woke. Good heavens—nearly time for dinner.

She took a shower, put on a clean dress and went down to the big lounge.

They were all there, chattering like a school treat, feeding themselves with their half-grapefruits. Kate collected hers from the long buffet table at the back of the room. One end of the table was piled with raw-vegetable salad in great bowls. She carefully stopped herself from taking any. In fact, she realized, she was tempted only because she was conventionally hungry. It was not real hunger, so it was not real temptation. She did, however, allow herself a long glass of boiled water, flavoured for a change with a slice of orange.

The Neals were seated by one of the long front windows. Kate took her ration to join them. They chatted affably, light-heartedly; never a hint of the realities of the afternoon.

A few minutes later she heard a greeting behind her. "Hallo, Kate."

"Henry," she said, turning, "where have you . . . ? Good heavens, what have you done to your head?"

It was circled by a neat bandage.

"Bumped it. I'll tell you later."

"Are you all right, darling?"

"Yes, quite all right."

"Well then," she said nervously, feeling upset, "you must meet Michael and Mary Neal. I've told you about them."

"I already knew you, of course, by repute, Mr. Neal," said Henry, taking a chair.

"You and your wife really are the nicest couple," Michael told him cosily. "How about joining us at dinner?"

Henry smiled. "I mustn't gorge. I had rather a late lunch. Otherwise, of course, I'd be delighted."

Kate could see that he was making a pretence, for civility. As soon as she could, therefore, she made the excuse that she must go to her room to rest.

"Come and talk to me for a while, Henry, so that I don't have to watch television."

3

As soon as they were in her room, she took hold of his arms. "Now, tell me."

"Don't fuss, darling. I'm quite all right. What happened was that when I went to my bedroom to wash for lunch I found that somebody had been searching through my papers. They were strewn all over the floor.

"The man must have ducked behind the door. When I went in, he hit me on the back of the head with the traditional blunt instrument. Knocked me out. By the time I came to, a few minutes later, he'd gone, of course."

"Henry, have you seen a doctor?"

"Yes. Toomey, the landlord, called in a white-haired old chap who seemed very efficient. He assured me there is no damage to the skull. I must have a thick one, he said, because the knock was none too gentle. All I got was a bump and a swelling. The doctor poulticed it and bandaged me up, and told me to rest all afternoon."

"Why didn't you phone me?"

"You'd simply have got into a fuss, and there was nothing you could do."

"Oh, Henry darling, I feel awful. I got you into this."

He laughed. "Don't fret. I tell you, I'm all right. I slept for three hours, then Mrs. Toomey brought me up some poached eggs on toast and a pot of coffee. The doctor came back at half past six, said the bump was subsiding nicely, and dressed it again. He said he was now sure there was nothing to worry about. So here I am."

"Have you told the police?"

"Not yet. That would be the worthy Sergeant Grey. Stoddart, the chap from Scotland Yard, is to be here for the Antrobus inquest tomorrow. Toomey told me he had booked a room at the Crown and will arrive late tonight. I'll tell him. I've an idea he'd prefer me to keep quiet about it."

"Why?"

"Well, it's fairly obvious, Kate, that somebody is desperate to get those damning evidence notes that Charles Pugh left in his case at the Crown, and which Stoddart himself now has—though only I know that. Pugh's house in London was broken into on Tuesday night. It could be coincidence, but I don't think it is. The bag was stolen from the Crown last night. Whoever took it found that the papers he wanted had been extracted. He must have thought I might have them. Since your story in the *Post*, darling, we've quite a reputation around here—the investigators! So he went to search my room, I interrupted him and he knocked me out."

"Who do you think it is?"

"If it weren't for the break-in at the London house, I'd say it was Charles Pugh himself. Those notes could now be more damning for him than for anybody."

"For him?"

"If he did return to Gorsedene on Monday night and kill Antrobus, those notes proclaim his motive. But he wouldn't have broken into his own house, and I can think of no reason why he should want to fake that break-in. So the person desperate to get those notes must be John Sherwood, and the actual intruder either Sherwood himself or, more probably, one of the thugs he's known to employ."

"Sherwood is here," Kate told him, lying down on the bed. "Michael and I overheard him having a row with Pelham Dimpsey. Sherwood wants to get at the documents left in Antrobus's room. I wonder if he's still searching for those evidence notes and thinks it possible that Pugh left them there."

"Shouldn't think so. Why wouldn't Dimpsey let him see them?"

"Orders from the police—Scotland Yard, via the Chief Constable."

"That'd be Stoddart, of course," said Henry. He switched on the lamp on the side table, for it was already twilight, and sat himself in the armchair by the window. Then he raised himself again, groped behind his back and pulled out a key tucked into the seat cushion. "You've left a key here."

"Key?" queried Kate. "I say, that must be the pass key to Antrobus's room. Charan Lal lent it to Mary Neal on the quiet. She was sitting there, and she was so agitated that she must have left it without realizing. I'll give it back to Mary in the morning, to return to Charan."

"Better do so before Stoddart gets here. Lal will have to surrender it. And what's all this about Mary Neal?"

Kate related the events of the afternoon.

Henry looked grave. "If we're making the assumption that Antrobus was murdered," he said, "it looks very like Michael Neal."

"I know. But it can't be. He's not that sort of man."

"Crazy to protect his wife? A sudden rage? An attack on impulse? Though I'm still damned if I can see what sort of attack it could have been."

"Henry, we're getting into a muddle. Let's assume murder, and forget the difficulties about method. And let's try to reconstruct that evening in Philip Antrobus's room, from what I heard, and what we've learned since."

He nodded. "Start with what you heard." He picked up the folder of Gorsedene notepaper from the writing table beside him and took out his pen. "I'll jot notes."

4

So, with Kate elaborating on any new fact of which Henry was unaware, they worked it out thus:

At about five o'clock on that Monday afternoon the helicopter returned with John Sherwood and he went into the house. Philip Antrobus was not on the terrace where everybody was taking a cup of tea. He was presumably in his room and there was no indication that he ever left it alive. He had already heard by telephone of the disaster on the Stock Exchange, and was probably starting to drink whisky.

At about 6:30 Kate talked to Charles Pugh, who was lifting his bag out of the helicopter and declaring his intention of chucking in his job. A few minutes later he got a message from Antrobus, and went up to his room. Say at about 6:40 Sherwood was still there, and had probably been there ever since his arrival. Kate did not know at what time Pugh left Gorsedene, but it was probably about seven o'clock. He took a taxi to the Crown and booked a room for the night.

It must have been about 7:30 when Phoebe Sadler (really Phoebe Antrobus) went to her ex-husband's room to negotiate about their young daughter, Rosabel. They argued for half an hour, but could not agree on a settlement. Phoebe wanted £20,000 to give up the child; he offered only £1,000. He told her that, if he had custody of Rosabel, the child would receive the insurance policy of £300,000 on his death. If he did not, he would cancel the policy and take the surrender value. Kate heard the angry end of this argument shortly before eight o'clock, when Antrobus walked out on to his balcony to flick a cigarette butt into the quadrangle below.

At 8:15 Phoebe must have gone, for Antrobus phoned Bella and told her to come to his room. She must go before a judge in chambers, he told her, and swear, falsely, that she supplied Phoebe with heroin; otherwise the police would be informed of her drug-peddling and bribery activities. Bella was terrified and forced to consent. She would get her instructions from Sherwood.

That interview was cut short by only a few minutes by Janet Dimpsey's arrival with a message from her husband about the business they had discussed earlier in the day. Kate did not know, of course, what the business was, but could guess with fair confidence that it was the question of closing or selling Gorsedene. Antrobus probably told the Dimpseys that his affairs were in such trouble that he could no longer keep the health farm going; arrangements he had had in mind for financing Pelham's takeover were now not practical; they would have to get out.

"And the message she delivered?" asked Henry.

"Perhaps Pelham had thought up some wild scheme as a possible alternative. Would Philip please defer any action until they had discussed that? I'm guessing, of course."

"Something of that kind," Henry agreed.

"Janet can't have stayed long," Kate continued, "because the next thing I heard, at eight forty-five, was laughter. I have the time exactly because it roused me from a doze and I looked at my travelling clock."

"Man or woman laughing?"

Kate confessed that she did not know. She had been only half awake. All she knew was that there had been laughter. Janet must have gone by then, for she had nothing to laugh about, and Antrobus would hardly be laughing at the plight of two old friends whose lives were to be desperately upset by the collapse of his own finances.

So somebody else must have gone to Antrobus's room after Janet had left. Who? Charles Pugh? No laughing matter there. Sherwood? Possibly.

"Michael Neal," said Henry.

Kate grimaced wryly but had to admit it was not impossible. Antrobus, already deep into the whisky bottle, might well have laughed at him.

"Then I heard nothing more until five past nine, checked again by glancing at my travelling clock," she went on. "There was an odd sort of tapping noise, then a thud."

"That thud seems to me to indicate that we're absolutely wrong, and it was suicide," said Henry. "The stool knocking against the bathroom wall as Antrobus kicked it away from under his feet."

"There are still my objections," defended Kate. "Why should a man about to kill himself go on a health cure? Why should a man hanging himself leave his door open for anyone to come in? And what did I see, or hear, or feel that makes the idea of suicide wrong?"

"Well, what?"

"I've thought and thought and I can't place it. The other consideration, of course, is all the people who had real motives for killing Philip Antrobus, all gathered together on the night he died."

"You think," asked Henry, "that they all did it, working as a team, like Dame Agatha's Orient Express murderers?"

"No, of course not. But I have a sort of instinctive conviction that is was murder, and one of them killed Antrobus."

"Let's list possibles, with their motives and opportunities," said Henry, selecting a fresh sheet of Gorsedene notepaper.

He listed them thus:

John Sherwood, to make sure of a very large profit from the Stock Exchange speculation, with which to bolt for a non-extradition country before the fraud came to light. He was staying at Gorsedene that night and could have gone to Antrobus's room at any time after Janet Dimpsey left, at 8:30 or a little later. Kate in fact saw him in the corridor at 9:50 and thought he had come from Antrobus's room.

Charles Pugh, in a semi-demented rage at discovering that Antrobus had hounded his father to death. He did not catch the evening train to London, as he had said he would, but booked in at the Crown, went out soon after dinner, and had not been seen since. He could easily have slipped up to Antrobus's room without being noticed. There were several entrances to the house, and only the front entrance was attended.

Michael Neal, because he was being blackmailed at his most sensitive point, his professional integrity, and threatened with a publication that would smear his young wife as involved in a vice racket. He admits he was in the room at some time before Kate found him and his wife at the door; that he then found Antrobus hanged, and so took the incriminating book typescript and tried to prevent his wife from returning it.

Charan Lal, perhaps accidentally in an attempt to kidnap Antrobus, to force him to remedy the monstrous condition in which Lal's people worked on the Antrobus tea plantations in Assam. Lal had a pass key and could have entered Antrobus's room at any time.

Phoebe and Eddie Sadler, to secure custody of the Antrobus child for Phoebe, and thus give them access to a trust of £300,000. Antrobus would certainly have admitted her if she had returned later with Eddie, saying they wanted to discuss further.

Janet Dimpsey who, so far as is at present known, was the last person to see Philip Antrobus alive. No apparent motive, for his death would have ensured the dissolution of Gorsedene. But nobody knows exactly what business the Dimpseys had been discussing earlier with Antrobus. And she was in the room during that evening.

Bella, because she was being threatened with the police and gaol. She also would have been admitted by Antrobus if she had returned to his room later.

Henry re-read his list slowly.

"I think we must strike out the two women who were there unaccompanied, Mrs. Dimpsey and Bella," he decided, "on the grounds of physical impossibility. I'm still doubtful whether it would have been possible for a man to have done it unaided. It would almost certainly need two."

"Which brings us to Phoebe and Eddie," said Kate.

"They are the most likely to have been able to have done the thing physically," Henry conceded. "And they had the strongest motive of all—money."

"So had John Sherwood, And how do we know he was unaided?" put in Kate. "If it was planned for the Stock Exchange thing, he could easily have planned for an accomplice."

"Point taken. And a good point, Kate. I reckon it puts Sherwood in the lead. He might even have had a double motive—something to do with the fraud in which he was involved. It's probably he who has been trying desperately to get hold of Charles Pugh's evidence notes, and now he's striving to get access to the Antrobus documents in the next room. Maybe there's something among them which would pin the fraud securely on him. It would have been typical of Antrobus's methods to have something to hold over his accomplice's head." He saw that Kate had sat up in bed and was tense. "What is it?"

She put a warning finger to her lips, then pointed to the window.

5

Henry turned his head. There was nothing to see. It was now quite dark outside, and the window pane simply reflected the inside of the room.

Then he heard a slight scraping noise. He looked at Kate. She nodded.

Henry rose silently, edged towards the window and peered out from behind the curtain. He glanced swiftly to the right, then down; and stepped back into the room.

"A man has just climbed to Antrobus's balcony," he told her in a quiet voice. "It's dead easy. There's a stackpile alongside, and a huge old wistaria trained against the wall. I caught only a glimpse of his back. He was putting a clasp knife to the french window. It opened at once, and he went in."

Kate was already off the bed.

"The key," she whispered urgently. "The pass key."

Henry, looking doubtful, picked up the key from the table where he had put it. "I don't like it, Kate."

"We must," she urged. "We simply must."

"All right," he reluctantly agreed. "But you stay here."

"Not on your nelly."

"Then I'll go in first, and you follow unless I shout to you to keep back."

He looked out into the corridor. It was empty.

It was only a few steps to the door to Antrobus's room. Kate was too close behind him. "Keep back," he muttered. But she did not obey.

Slowly he pushed the key into the lock, twisted it gingerly. The door gently yielded.

He thrust the door open and stepped inside.

A man in dark jersey and slacks was nervously emptying the wallets on to the table, scanning their contents with a flashlight, working fast, evidently sure of what he sought.

The opening of the door did not instantly alert him. He was concentrating too hard. But he suddenly realized that he had been interrupted. He swung the beam of the flashlight round, rushed at Henry and clipped him on the jaw, knocking him down backwards.

Kate was standing in the doorway. The man caught her

by the arm, jerked her swiftly into the room and shoved her against the bed, across which she sprawled.

The room went dark as the man dowsed his torch. Then he was gone into the corridor.

Kate scrambled off the bed, switched on the bedside light and ran to the door. The corridor was empty. The man could have sped down any of the three staircases, including the service stairs.

She turned into the room and knelt by Henry. "Are you all right?"

"Last time it was a knockout," he said ruefully. "If I'm not damn careful, I'll lose this round on points. It's all right, Kate. All I got was a crack on the jaw. No real damage done, except to my manly pride. He packs a very useful right, whoever he is."

"I believe I know who he is," she said slowly. "Of course, I can't be quite sure. There was only the light of that torch, and his face was in shadow behind it. But I'm fairly certain it was Charles Pugh."

CHAPTER 13

EARLY ON Friday morning Kate was woken by Janet Dimpsey.

"We're re-arranging everything this morning, Mrs. Theobald, because of the inquest. My husband has to attend, of course, and so, I suppose, do you."

"At eleven. I had a word yesterday with the girls downstairs, and they agreed to give me my steam bath at nine, and massage at half past."

"Yes, they've made the alterations in today's schedule. The difficulty is that you were to have had a consultation with my husband at twelve noon, and of course that can't be managed now. He can see you, either late this afternoon or, if you prefer, as early as possible this morning, before your treatments begin."

Kate looked at her clock. It was only a quarter to eight.

"If you will have my grapefruit sent up straight away, Mrs. Dimpsey, I'll be in the director's room by half past eight. Okay? Good. How are you, by the way? I hope you haven't had any more migraine."

She still looked haggard, and the cosmetics were even heavier than before.

"I'm all right now," Janet answered. "I had a slight touch of headache last night, but that usually happens. After a severe bout, there's a secondary a few days later, not nearly as bad. Then it clears away." She tried to smile. "So I hope I'm through with it for a while. And Pelham has put me back on the herbal regimen. It worked pretty well before. I'll tell Pelham, then, to expect you at half past eight."

144

She had gone without saying anything about the man who had broken into Antrobus's room during the night. That must mean that the police were keeping quiet about it. Henry had gone back to the Crown to find the Scotland Yard man, Stoddart, and report to him. Stoddart had obviously said nothing of it to the Dimpseys. Kate wondered why.

The maid arrived with her half-grapefruit and boiled water. Kate switched on the radio, but switched off again when she found she was listening to the eight o'clock news bulletin. She still had two more days' holiday from news.

Pelham Dimpsey was waiting for her. He, too, she thought, was showing the effects of the strain to which he had been subjected this week. The clear whiteness of his eyes was slightly bloodshot, and the pouches beneath the eyes had darkened. But he retained his suave, professional, extremely polite manner as he studied his preliminary diagnosis of her, then the reports during the week.

"I think the treatments have benefited you a great deal, Mrs. Theobald."

"Oddly enough, I feel fine."

He smiled gently and gave his routine discourse on the benefits of fasting at regular intervals. Then he took her blood pressure, examined her eyes, her throat, deferentially put a few questions about bowel movements and sleeping experience, and at last asked her to step on the scales.

"Admirable," he murmured. "You have achieved what we hoped for."

"Glory be!"

"In fact, you have slightly surpassed our hopes. Today and tomorrow you should eat a plateful of raw-vegetable salad at one meal at least, at both mid-day and in the evening if you wish."

"But won't that start to put on the ounces?"

He smiled. "Not noticeably. And you should begin to eat more, in preparation for leaving here. It would be dangerous to follow a grapefruit diet with an ordinary solid meal."

"Salad," she murmured. "Raw vegetables. How delicious!"

"I trust that anything more you write about Gorsedene, Mrs. Theobald," he said diffidently, "will be of its therapeutic benefits rather than its misfortunes."

"Anything I write about Gorsedene as a health cure will be ecstatic," she assured him. "But does it really matter any more? Publicity for the place, I mean. Isn't it likely to close?"

Pelham Dimpsey sighed. "Who can say, as yet? I have consulted my lawyer and my accountant, and apparently there is a faint hope that I might be able to take over, once poor Philip's affairs are in the hands of a liquidator. But I regard that hope as slender. Janet and I have been discussing our future at length, and it is probable that we shall decide to try our fortunes in America."

"Then Michael Neal . . . "

Dimpsey nodded. "Mr. Neal has spoken to me about it. He has assured me that any financial problems of setting up a Gorsedene in the States would be solved with ease, and has most kindly promised me his help, if I decide on that course." He sighed again. "But to leave here . . . Ah well."

"I'll see you at the inquest then," said Kate. "I shan't be reporting that, since I have to give evidence. The *Post* is sending another reporter to cover it—and so, I imagine, is nearly every newspaper in Christendom."

She was surprised, when she went down to the bathhouse, to find all the cabinets already occupied, all the female heads nodding and chatting vigorously.

"Everybody is very early this morning," she remarked to Phyllis as she was helped into her own cabinet.

"You bet," answered Bella, her smiling head, topknot secured, protruding from the neighbouring cabinet. She seemed as jolly as usual, with no sign of the nerves of the previous afternoon. "Nobody's going to miss the inquest."

"I doubt if you'll get in," said Kate. "There must be a queue already, and the court room will barely hold the reporters."

Which was about right, Henry told her when he arrived to drive her to the inquest. The little town was swarming with reporters. Toomey had never done such business. He had men sleeping on his billiards table, on corridor floors, in a workshop across the yard, and in a disused stable. "And he's talking with awe of his bar takings."

"You told the police about our break-in last night?"

"Yes. Stoddart was at the Crown when I got back. He told me not to speak of it to anybody. He must be on to something."

"He can't have reported it to Gorsedene," said Kate. "I saw both the Dimpseys this morning and they didn't mention it. So they can't have known anything about it."

Henry shrugged. "That's up to the police."

2

The coroner's court was already packed full when they arrived, but Sergeant Grey met them to escort Kate to the bench reserved for witnesses. He told Henry there was no room for him.

"I am a member of the Bar, Sergeant, and I hold a watching brief for Mrs. Theobald. I shall require a place at the lawyers' table." He handed Sergeant Grey his card. "Be good enough, please, to deliver this to the coroner."

Kate smiled appreciatively.

Sergeant Grey, taken aback, pointed reluctantly to the well of the court. There were already several men there—solicitors with their clerks, Henry told her, and a couple of barristers whom he knew, eminent men, obviously looking after the Antrobus interests. He joined them, and Kate joined the witnesses, sitting next to Pelham Dimpsey, who gave her a despondent smile.

The coroner took his seat on the high dais at the far end of the court. He was a thin, precise, elderly man.

"Is he a doctor?" she asked Pelham.

"No, a solicitor. Mr Grantley. He is well thought of locally. An excellent man. Nothing escapes him."

Kate had reservations about that, as far as her own evidence was concerned.

She glanced round the court. The Press table could not accommodate all the reporters. Several whom she recognized were jammed on to the public benches. Bella, she saw, had managed to push her way into the back row, grinning cheerfully. The Neals had evidently arrived early enough to get seats near the front.

Kate was the first to be called. She mounted the varnished oak steps to the witness box, took the oath and related how she had left her room a few minutes before 10:30 on that Monday evening, to find a coinbox phone. She wanted to talk to her husband in London, and could get no answer from the Gorsedene switchboard. The door to the neighbouring room, which she knew Mr. Philip Antrobus occupied, was ajar, so she went in.

"Why did you go into that room, Mrs. Theobald?" asked the coroner. He had a thin, high voice, almost a squeak.

Kate looked demure. "Just curiosity, I'm afraid, sir. I'm a newspaper reporter. We're an incurably inquisitive lot."

She glanced quickly at the Press table, catching a few grins. She knew most of the men, of course. Dereck Andrews, from the *Recorder*, her staunchest friend on Fleet Street, was looking, she was amused to see, a little shocked.

"Very well, Mrs. Theobald," said the coroner. "Pray continue."

So she related how she entered the room, the door to the bathroom was ajar and she could see a man's legs dangling in the air. She ventured to the bathroom door, saw that it was Mr. Antrobus, hanging from a pipe across the ceiling by a cord round his neck. Yes, she later saw that it was the cord from the dressing-gown he was wearing, a rather flamboyant, unusual gown.

"And then, Mrs. Theobald?"

Then she clutched at the telephone by the bedside. Mr. Pelham Dimpsey, the Gorsedene director, answered her call. He came hurrying to the room and she assisted him to get Mr. Antrobus's body down by cutting the cord above his head. Then Mr. Dimpsey and she laid the body on the bed and Mr. Dimpsey telephoned for a doctor and the police.

"And that's really all I can tell the court."

None of the lawyers wanted to question her, so she returned to her seat.

Pelham Dimpsey was called next. Kate could see how desperately nervous he was, but he took the oath with dignity, forcing himself to be calm. There was quality in the man.

He told of the events of the evening, from the moment when, passing through the main entrance hall of Gorsedene, and noticing that the porter must have been called away and had left the switchboard unmanned, he had answered Mrs. Theobald's call.

To Kate's astonishment, Henry rose and announced that he held a watching brief for Mrs. Kate Theobald.

"For your wife, Mr. Theobald?" asked the coroner. "Isn't that rather irregular?"

"There was no time to make other arrangements. Have I your permission to question this witness?"

"Yes, if you wish."

Henry turned to the witness box. "Mr. Dimpsey, when you arrived in Mr. Antrobus's room that night, in response to the telephone call from Mrs. Theobald, did she seem to you shocked and astonished?"

"Oh certainly. Very shocked."

"And astonished?"

"Why, yes. She had just made this gruesome discovery . . ."

"Thank you," said Henry, sitting down.

Kate wondered why he had intervened, then gasped as she took in the reason. If there were ever to be suspects, he was establishing that she had just gone into that room, and was not among them. It had not occurred to her before that she could be; but, of course, she clearly could.

Another barrister rose. He informed the coroner that he held a watching brief for a committee that had been formed to represent shareholders in Antrobus Enterprises Limited. The coroner uneasily queried the relevance to this enquiry. But the barrister was a Queen's Counsel of such eminence, and a man of so commanding a presence, and he gave the coroner such a cold stare, that he received permission to question the witness.

The questions established that Pelham Dimpsey had a long personal and business relationship with the deceased; that the deceased was, in effect, his employer. Further questions delved into Philip Antrobus's handling of the business interests in Gorsedene.

At first Kate could not see what the lawyer was driving at, but then she began to have a vague idea that he was trying to establish commercial malpractices by Antrobus. Maybe there were some personal resources that the shareholders could make claim for, if it could be shown that the company's disaster was caused by criminal guilt on the part of its chairman. It sounded like the start of a long, costly legal battle.

Kate grimaced. To begin at the inquest on the man's corpse seemed somehow indecent.

Dimpsey was followed on the witness stand by Sergeant Grey, who gave a plodding account of his part in Monday evening's proceedings. Nobody wanted to question Sergeant Grey.

The doctor should have come next, but the coroner's officer reported that Dr. Williams had been summoned away to an emergency—a complicated delivery in the hospital's maternity ward. He craved the indulgence of the court and would return as soon as humanly possible.

The coroner remarked that birth must take precedence over death, glancing at the Press table as though inviting them to report his witticism; the local newspaper certainly would.

Meanwhile there was one more witness to give evidence. Mr. John Sherwood was called.

3

The point of calling him was, of course, to establish Philip Antrobus's state of mind on the Monday evening. Sherwood left little doubt about that. During the morning there had been extraordinary selling of the Antrobus Enterprise stock. He had at once telephoned Mr. Antrobus, who was deeply worried, but instructed him not to buy the shares in, but to await events.

"By midday the situation had worsened badly. There was wild selling, and inevitably all sorts of rumours went about the City concerning Antrobus Enterprises' affairs."

"Were the rumours well founded?" asked the coroner.

Sherwood hesitated. "That is a difficult question to answer, sir. In the present economic climate all large and complicated holding companies are at some risk. Antrobus Enterprises was no exception."

"You kept Mr. Antrobus informed throughout the day of the state of the market?"

"Oh yes. We were in touch by telephone all day. When the market closed, he instructed me to fly to Gorsedene in the firm's helicopter, bringing him various documents and reports that he would need to assess the exact gravity of the situation."

"In what state of mind did you find him?"

"Perturbed at first, naturally, sir. But not unduly so. Then, as he began to appreciate the full extent of the disaster—it was nothing less—he became very agitated and distressed. He also started to drink a lot of whisky. That was most unusual for Mr. Antrobus at a time of crisis."

The rest of his evidence related that their conference was interrupted by the helicopter pilot, a Mr. Charles Pugh, who wished to give notice to leave his employment. Sherwood did not know the reason, but supposed that Mr. Pugh had received an offer for a better job elsewhere.

"It was not a good moment, however, to approach Mr. Antrobus. He flew into a rage and abused Mr. Pugh vigorously. He told him, in very obscene language, to clear off straight away, and swore he would get no pay for that month—to which, of course, Mr. Pugh was legally entitled. But Mr. Antrobus was in a confused and irrational state, and he was getting rather intoxicated. Mr. Pugh went off, and I left the room soon after."

"And that was the last you saw of your employer alive?"

Sherwood nodded and muttered that that was so. He seemed to be slightly choked with emotion.

Queen's Counsel rose.

"Mr. Sherwood, you were Mr. Antrobus's right-hand man in his business affairs?"

"I was one of his business advisers."

"You had been in his confidence since the early stages of his career?"

"Partly in his confidence."

"Are you of the opinion that the financial insecurity of Antrobus Enterprises Limited, as revealed by events on the Stock Exchange on that day, led Mr. Antrobus to take his own life?"

Sherwood hesitated. Then he said, "I don't think there can be any other interpretation."

"Now, Mr. Sherwood, this is not the place to enter into details of either the financial circumstances of Antrobus Enterprises Limited, or of the Stock Exchange transactions on that Monday. But perhaps you will give us some general information about either."

"If I can."

"As to the financial state of the company, would you agree that there could be any substance in persistent rumours in the City that certain irregularities, shall be say, were about to come to light?"

"Nothing of the kind. The danger was simply the usual one these days, that the company had borrowed short in order to finance long-term operations, and if there were panic, the banks might call in those short-term loans."

"Thank you, Mr. Sherwood." There was obvious sarcasm in Counsel's voice. "Now, some thirteen years ago were you engaged with Mr. Antrobus in forming a financial syndicate that began operations in commodity markets, and later extended into general investment?"

"There was such a syndicate. But Mr. Antrobus and I disassociated ourselves from it about ten years ago."

"The Stock Exchange dealings on that Monday amounted, would you agree, to what is called, in City jargon, a bear raid?"

"It seemed like it."

"That is, somebody was selling large quantities of Antrobus Enterprises stock which he did not own, in the hope—or perhaps with the benefit of inside knowledge, with the certainty—that he could buy them at a much lower figure before settling day, and pocket the balance?"

"That is a bear raid, of course."

"Are you aware that the chief operator in that bear raid was the syndicate to which I have just referred?"

Sherwood shrugged. "I cannot know who was buying or

selling our shares until the certificates reach the company offices in due course, for transfer."

"Unless, covertly, you were using that syndicate as a tool for your own speculative activities?"

Sherwood stared at him: "That is a disgraceful and unworthy suggestion."

"I think," the coroner said to Counsel, "that that question not only lacks relevance to this present enquiry but, as Counsel is aware, of course, it is of a nature that might prove incriminating, and therefore I cannot permit it."

Counsel inclined his head. "If it pleases you, I agree that these questions might more appropriately be pursued in some other place. I have nothing more to ask this witness."

Kate watched Sherwood closely as he left the witness stand and resumed his seat. He showed not the slightest apprehension. Whatever else, the man had nerve.

Dr. Williams was now ascending the steps to the witness box.

He gave his medical evidence in simple form, aware that the coroner was a lawyer and not a doctor. He had found the body laid out on the bed, where Mr. Dimpsey and Mrs. Theobald had placed it. The cord by which, they informed him, it had been hanging, was no longer round the neck, but there were marks and contusions. Death had occurred through respiratory failure, caused by constriction of the gullet and windpipe by pressure around the neck—what, in common parlance, is called strangulation.

"I had hastened to Gorsedene," he said, "when Pelham Dimpsey telephoned to me, as he had expressed his hope that I might be able to resuscitate his patient. But there was no chance of that, as I appreciated directly I examined the body. Death had occurred at least an hour previously, probably sooner."

"At what time did you examine the body, Dr. Williams?" asked the coroner.

"By my wrist watch, which is reasonably accurate, I started my examination at ten fifty-three p.m."

"So death must have occurred before, say, nine-fifty?"

"At the very latest. It could have occurred half an hour or even one hour earlier. I would estimate that it took place not earlier than, say, half past eight o'clock that evening, and not later than a quarter before ten o'clock."

He then, presumably for the record, consulted some notes and started on a detailed medical report on the cause of death.

As he did so, Kate was staring at him, seeing once more that tableau in Philip Antrobus's room: the doctor bending over the corpse on the bed, the skirt of the vivid dressing-gown draped over its edge and trailing on the floor; Sergeant Grey and Pelham Dimpsey entering the bathroom; Dr. Williams unloosing the pyjamas beneath the dressing-gown, listening to the naked chest, straightening to move his hands along to the head twisted on the bedcover, the protruding tongue, the livid throat.

Suddenly Kate tautened, put a knuckle to her mouth, touching it with her teeth.

At last she knew what she had seen that was wrong.

CHAPTER 14

As HE LISTENED to the inquest, Henry grew steadily more convinced that Antrobus had committed suicide. The evidence was overwhelming. He had been led by Kate's imagination into contemplating the possibility of murder. That was nonsense. At a crisis in his personal as well as his business affairs, the man had hanged himself.

It would have been more satisfactory, he considered, in view of the widespread consequences of Antrobus's death, if the coroner had adjourned this inquest in order to summon a jury. He had no need to, of course. Like all lawyers, Henry disapproved of the almost unlimited powers which coroners have acquired over the centuries, even though they seldom use them.

But no jury, he admitted to himself, could have come to any other verdict than that which the coroner was now pronouncing—suicide while the balance of mind was disturbed. There was no reason for the addition about the balance of mind, since suicide had not been a criminal offense since 1953, but old-fashioned coroners kept on including the phrase.

As for the need of a jury, the coroner was now dealing with that. He had been undecided, he was saying, as to whether he should adjourn this inquest for a jury to hear. But when he read the statements preliminary to evidence, it had seemed to him that no jury could possibly differ from the verdict he had just given. It had seemed to him preferable, then, in view of the magnitude of commercial matters which, he understood, were involved, to reach a definite verdict as soon as possible.

The court rose.

Henry started to edge through the crowd towards Kate

when Sergeant Grey touched his arm. Detective Chief Superintendent Stoddart would be obliged if Mr. Theobald would step along to see him. "He's in the coroner's officer's room, sir."

"All right. But I'd better arrange for my wife to get back to Gorsedene. I was going to drive her."

He got to Kate and told her that Stoddart wanted to see him. Would she like to take the car?

"No. You keep it. You'll need it to get out to Gorsedene, and come as quickly as you can, because I've something important to tell you. I'll cadge a lift. Oh, Mr. Dimpsey, are you going back by car? Can you take me? My husband has to stay in the town for a while."

"Of course, Mrs. Theobald."

As she turned away, Kate repeated over her shoulder, "Come quickly. It really is important."

Sergeant Grey took him to a room at the rear where Stoddart was waiting.

"Can you spare me an hour to come to the station and look at some photographs?"

"By all means. About last night?"

He glanced questioningly at Sergeant Grey.

"It's all right," said Stoddart, "Sergeant Grey knows the circumstances. For the moment, however, we're not letting on about it generally. But I think the man may be known to the police, so I've had the relevant photographs brought down here this morning, in the hope that you may be able to recognize him."

"I'll try, though I had such an unsatisfactory look at his face. The only light in the room was the torch the man was holding, and he shone it directly into my eyes as he rushed me."

When they reached the police station, Henry looked at the thick bundle of photographs on the desk.

"He was a burly man," he said, "strongly built, and, I'd say a little less than six feet tall."

"That should eliminate quite a few," Stoddart agreed, reading the particulars attached to each picture, rejecting those which did not fit, and passing the others slowly, one by one, to Henry.

He stared at each for a minute or two. Most he handed

back to Stoddart, murmuring, "Not that one." Now and then he laid one aside on the desk.

It took more than an hour to get through the bundle. By then, Henry had reserved seven photographs. He gave each of these a second scrutiny, shading the picture with his hand to simulate shadow.

At last he picked out three, rejecting the others.

"It just might be one of these," he said. "But I can't be anything like certain. It's almost a guess. I saw the man's face so dimly. I'm afraid I'm not being of much use to you, Mr. Stoddart."

The policeman stretched over and picked up one of the three photographs.

"On the contrary, most helpful. This man is an employee of one of the Antrobus firms. He's supposed to be a guard at a warehouse. In fact, he's not often there. We know he's one of John Sherwood's strong-arm men. Suggestive at least, eh, Mr. Theobald?"

"I couldn't possibly give evidence of identification. You do appreciate that?"

"Of course. But it gives us something to work on."

"Are you going to ask my wife to look at the photos? She saw the man, too, possibly a little more clearly than I did."

"I don't think I need trouble her at present. We'll work on this man for a bit. I expect to find enough to put pressure on him."

"Come to think of it," said Henry, "Kate wouldn't agree with my choice. Directly the man had gone, she said she thought she had recognized him. As I told you last night, she thought he was Charles Pugh. Of course, she also saw him only in a very difficult light."

"She was mistaken. It could not have been Pugh."

"You've traced him?"

"Not by police action. We had a stroke of luck. Two local boys were out bird-nesting early this morning. They noticed a stray dog sniffing about in some bushes at the bottom of a disused quarry about a mile outside the town, not the Gorsedene side, but to the south. They went to look. In the undergrowth they saw a man's body. It was Charles Pugh."

"Good heavens!"

"The boys ran to the nearest house, and the householder telephoned the station. The sergeant and I drove out. That man hadn't intruded anywhere last night. He had been dead for several days."

"You're sure it was Pugh?"

"I came back to the Crown to find Sherwood and he drove out with me, and identified the body at once."

"What had happened?"

"It looks as though he fell over the lip of the quarry and struck his head on the rock outcrops below. His forehead was knocked in badly. It was a fracture of the skull, Dr. Williams says, that killed him. That disused quarry is supposed to be fenced round the top. But the fencing has rotted and broken away at the point where Pugh fell."

"You think he fell into the quarry on Monday evening, which is why he never returned to the Crown?"

"Probably."

"What was he doing, wandering about in the woods at night, a mile outside the town?"

"Who can say?" asked Stoddart. "Taking an evening stroll, maybe, to cool his temper."

2

Kate was waiting impatiently in her room for Henry. Why didn't he come? What did the police want to see him about?

Then he telephoned. "I've been at the police station all this time."

"Why?"

"I'll tell you when we meet. Interesting. No, you'll have to wait until I get there. I'm not talking about it on the phone."

"I'll die of curiosity."

He laughed. "Try to contain it until after lunch. I'm going back to the Crown for something to eat. I'm ravenous."

"*You're* ravenous!"

He laughed again. "Sorry. I'm peckish, so I'm going

back to the Crown for a light snack. Enjoy your grapefruit."

"It's not going to be grapefruit. Pelham Dimpsey told me this morning that I must prepare for my return to the greedy world by eating something more substantial."

"Such as?"

"Raw-vegetable salad."

She was so irritated by his laughter that she hung up. When she reached the dining-room she found herself queuing for salad just behind Michael Neal.

"Have they let you off too?"

He turned round, then smiled. "Pelham Dimpsey thinks we should have what he calls a square meal before we get back to Washington. Did I tell you, we're off early tomorrow. I've arranged a car to drive us to Heathrow. So, allowing for the time change, we'll be home for lunch. Mary is already listing in her mind what she has that's most succulent in the freezer. Our first proper meal for a week—oh boy! You can't count what we'll eat on the journey. All that coloured airline plastic served on little cardboard trays. Still, I suppose anything'll taste good for a couple of days."

"Not so tasty as raw grated carrot and turnip slices," said Kate. "Your turn at the salad."

He piled a couple of plates ecstatically. Kate took her turn, then followed him to the table by the window where Mary awaited them.

For several minutes they made no sound except the champing of lettuce, the sharp snap of a bitten carrot, a chewing of radishes and of shredded cabbage.

There was no dressing on the salad and it was devoid of salt. At Gorsedene, eating salt was the eighth deadly sin, even more heinous than drinking coffee. But Kate could not recall ever having enjoyed a dish more fully. A quick glance at the Neals, both absorbed in mastication, was enough to show that they were having the same experience.

At last Michael sighed, and they all took a rest.

"Dee-licious," he declared. And both women nodded with satisfaction.

Michael took a swig at the boiled water (lemon flavour).

"I tried jumping Charan with that story of the tea plantations," he told Kate. "He reacted quite normally—admitted that he was the leader of the protesters, and added that he, for one, was glad that Antrobus had hanged himself. I'm sure, though, that there's nothing in your idea that he was involved in Antrobus's death. So that's tidied up before we leave. Now, how about that book and the articles?"

"I have them safe."

"You told me you thought there was somebody who could still use the material for blackmail. But I've taken care of that. My London lawyer has made preliminary soundings with the Antrobus publishing house about buying the firm's copyrights. He's hinting he's acting for another publisher of porn. First reactions are favourable."

"All the same," reasoned Kate, "if a potential blackmailer got hold of a copy—and there must be at least a couple in that publishing house—he could still turn the screw on you. Copyright wouldn't help."

"Who are you thinking of?"

"John Sherwood."

"He has access to the publishing office, of course," Michael mused. "But do you think a man of his standing would risk blackmail, not for the sort of reason that Antrobus had, but just for money?"

"By what I hear, he'd do almost anything for money."

"He'd have to know there was something in that publishing office to look for."

"That's your best hope," Kate agreed, "that he doesn't know what sort of pressure his boss was putting on you."

Mary sat there in silence, but in such distress that she was on the edge of tears. Michael leaned forward and put his hand on hers.

"Don't fret, honey. It probably won't happen. If it does, I'll know how to deal with it, now that the senator isn't involved." He turned to Kate. "In any event, the typescript you have can't help Sherwood, or anybody else. I'd certainly like to have that, to destroy."

"Very well. I'll give it to you when we meet for our cup of tea. If I miss you at tea—Henry's coming round, and we may go for a walk—I'll see you at 'cocktail hour.' "

Michael grinned. "Happy thought. At that time tomorrow—ignoring the five-hours-back—I'll be sipping the first martini to pass my lips since, it feels like, Christmas twelvemonth."

"Gin and tonic for me," said Kate. "Then Henry's taking me out to a carefully chosen, very expensive dinner."

3

Henry was standing by the door of her room.

"What did the policeman want?" she asked, admitting him.

Henry took the chair by the window while Kate lodged herself on the bed.

"I had to go through a lot of photographs, trying to identify last night's intruder. In spite of the dim look I had at him, it turned out that one of three I whittled it down to is an Antrobus employee, and known to be used by Sherwood for dirty work."

"It does sound too apt to be coincidence," Kate agreed. "If it isn't, then Sherwood must be desperate to get hold of something among those documents. Do you think he'll try again tonight?"

"He's too late. At Stoddart's request the county police impounded them while we were at the inquest. They have a magistrate's order which permits them to hold the papers while allegations of fraud are being investigated."

"So you think Sherwood is trapped?"

"Could be."

If so, she thought, Michael Neal need not worry any more. She would tell him as much when she gave him the typescript.

"Mind you," said Henry, "the identification of last night's intruder is still just guesswork."

"Did you tell Stoddart I thought the man was Charles Pugh?"

"Yes. But he wasn't. That's the news I have for you."

He told her of the discovery of Pugh's body.

Kate stared at him. "Then that clinches it, Henry."

"Clinches what?"

"Antrobus's murder."

"He killed himself," said Henry firmly.

"No, no. Surely now it's obvious. Pugh came back to Gorsedene, killed Antrobus in a rage, then ran off through the woods, half demented—and went over the edge of that quarry. It could have been deliberate. Coming to his senses, he might have chosen that, rather than risk a murder trial and life imprisonment. But it could just as easily have been accident. The guard rail was rotted and broken, you said."

"Now listen, Kate. During the inquest I thought the whole thing out objectively, as though you were really only my client and not my wife. The inquest verdict was correct. Antrobus hanged himself. For anybody, no matter how strong, to have overcome Antrobus and strung him up to that pipe in the bathroom is a physical impossibility. Even if Antrobus were half drunk—or quite drunk, if you like—it couldn't have been done without making such a row that you would certainly have heard it in the next room. It has been an amusing game, that's all, trying to construct a murder mystery out of it. But it wasn't. It was suicide."

Kate was smiling. "But Henry, it wasn't. I told you that I've realized what I saw that was wrong. While Dr. Williams was giving his evidence, the whole scene in that room, that night, came up in my mind like a coloured photograph. And I saw once again what was wrong, and this time I pin-pointed it."

"Well, what was wrong?" he asked indulgently.

"The mark round the neck, Henry. It was in the wrong place."

"How do you mean?"

"When I saw the body hanging, the noose of the dressing-gown cord went under his jaw, then round the neck to the back of his head. When I saw the body on the bed, with the doctor examining it, the strangulation mark was lower down, at least an inch lower, round the throat."

"What are you suggesting?"

"That Antrobus was strangled, probably from behind, without warning, and probably not with that dressing gown cord, while he was still in his bedroom. Then, to make it look like suicide, the man, whoever it was, looped the cord round his neck and hauled him up to that pipe."

"You think he was first garrotted, then strung up after he was dead?"

"Garrotted!" she exclaimed excitedly. "Thuggee. India. Famous for it. India. Charan Lal."

Henry laughed. "Come off it, Kate. Five minutes ago you were sure that Charles Pugh murdered Antrobus. Now it's the Indian porter. Keep going, darling. You'll soon be able to make it work for everyone on that funny list of suspects we drew up. It's nonsense, Kate. Even granting the garrotting theory—which I don't—it would still have needed remarkable physical strength to hang a dead body on that pipe. Philip Antrobus hanged himself."

"But the mark on the neck," she objected.

"Either the cord, or more likely your memory of the scene slipped. It was suicide."

"I think you should tell the policeman about the mark on the neck."

"I should simply look a fool, especially after the inquest verdict."

"It wouldn't hurt to tell Stoddart about the mark, and you could say it's my idea, and you pooh-pooh it. But tell him. I know I'm right about it."

"I'll think about that," he told her indulgently.

"If you don't tell him, I shall. But think about it somewhere else, there's a darling. I need an hour's rest after that vast lunch. How delicious it was! I still have the exquisite taste of crunchy raw carrot on my tongue."

Rising, he kissed her carefully on the cheek.

"And the exquisite taste of garlic," he assured her.

4

When he had gone, she tried to doze, but could not. Her mind was too busily engaged. When she closed her eyes, she saw again those two vivid pictures—the corpse hanging in the bathroom, and the corpse lying on the bed. The mark on the neck *was* in the wrong place.

But she had to admit that Henry's further objection was

valid. How could anybody drag a dead man from the bedroom into the bathroom, and then haul him up to that pipe by the dressing-gown cord?

She went into her own bathroom, to stare at the pipe across the ceiling. The body would have to be lifted well off the floor before the cord round the neck could be threaded over the pipe, for the cord could not be more than about a yard and a half in length. Alternatively the cord, with the noose already made, would have to be secured to the pipe, and then the body lifted high enough to thrust the lolling head through the loop.

Kate sighed. It was virtually impossible for anyone to have done it, either way. Two men would be needed; just possibly a man and a woman, which returned her thoughts to Eddie and Phoebe Sadler.

But then, what about Charles Pugh? Could coincidence really stretch so far as Pugh, in a murderous rage against Antrobus, falling to his death at the same time as Phoebe and Eddie killed the man? Preposterous!

It was no use going back on to her bed. She would take a walk.

She went down to the front terrace, which had not yet filled for tea. The Neals were there, also just about to take a walk. She asked them if they were coming along the river bank, but Michael said they were taking the shorter way down the Gorsedene drive to the entrance gates, because then they must start packing.

So Kate left them and crossed the wide lawn to the river's edge. But soon she found the sun too hot. She felt lethargic. So she turned towards the golf links, strolled the length of the first three holes, then cut across the fairway, back towards the house.

As she entered the big vegetable garden, she smiled to herself. All that lovely salad—grown here, doubtless without the aid of chemicals, but only compost. Over there in the kitchen girls must already be shelling walnuts and peas, and shredding cabbage and turnips in preparation for her evening meal. She might even be allowed a small wedge of cheese.

She went on into the quadrangle at the rear of the house.

The usual bikinis were stretched out in the sunshine round the pool, the usual stout, ageing men eyeing them covetously, or occasionally plunging into the water to swim a few gentle strokes and cool off.

Kate strolled on towards the stable yard. A girl was dismounting, a groom taking the reins to lead her pony into a stall. A lorry that had put down a load of big sacks of feed started up and drove off down the entrance drive. One of the stable hands was fastening a sack on to a block and tackle, and hoisting it to the open door of the grain store above, where another man pulled it in and unhooked it.

Kate suddenly checked in her stride. That sack must weigh at least a hundredweight. The man in the yard, having fastened the hook, was hauling a second sack upwards with complete ease and small effort. Aside from a slight squeaking as the rope passed over the pulley wheel above, there was no noise.

A block and tackle. Anyone could use it—even a woman.

She went up to the stable hand, smiling cheerfully.

"That's a useful gadget you've got there," she remarked conversationally, "for lifting heavy weights."

"It's quite ordinary, miss. It's what everybody uses for this kind of job. It's called a block and tackle. Hooks and pulley wheels—they take the weight. All I've got to do is pull on this rope."

"Could I do it?"

"Course you could, miss. Want to try?"

"I'll take your word for it. The one you're using looks new."

"That's right. We had to get a new one, because somebody walked off with the old one."

"Recently?"

"A few days ago." He called up to the man aloft. "When did we miss the old block and tackle, Fred?"

"Tuesday."

"That's right. It was here Monday afternoon, miss. When we came in on Tuesday morning, it'd gone. We got it back, though. When did we get it back, Fred? Wednesday, wasn't it?"

"'Sright. Wednesday."

"Charan found it," the stable hand told her. "The Indian porter chap. Found it some place, he said—out in the woods, I think. Funny thing to steal, eh, a block and tackle? And then just to chuck it down in the woods? I think he said he found it in the woods. Oh, there he is now."

Kate turned and saw Charan Lal walking past the entrance to the yard, making towards the gymnasium building.

"Hey, Charan," the stable hand yelled, "where was it you found the old block and tackle, then? Out in the woods, was it? Lady here asking about it."

From the suddenness with which Lal halted, and the glance he sent at her, Kate at once understood that, at last, she knew; and Charan Lal knew that she knew.

He had turned and was coming towards them.

"Yes, Alf," he said softly, "in the woods, down by the little stream, where the fallen oak tree is. Why did you ask, Mrs. Theobald?"

She smiled and shrugged her shoulders. "I didn't, really. I was just admiring the easy way in which the grain was being hoisted, and our friend here told me that somebody had walked off with the block and tackle, and you found it."

She realized that her voice was tailing off.

"Ah well," she said, as brightly as she could, "I must go and get ready for tea. Do I get cake today, Charan? I've been taken off the regimen diet, you know."

"I don't think there'll be cake, Mrs. Theobald," he answered, still in a quiet voice.

"I'll get ready all the same," she said, turning to walk through the car park, whence she could round the house to the front terrace.

As she went through the car park, she had an uneasy feeling that he was following her.

She dared not turn to look. She tried to increase her pace a little, without seeming to hurry too much. She was damn scared.

He came up behind her so swiftly and silently that the

first indication she had was the touch of his hand on her arm.

"Keep walking, Mrs. Theobald."

She felt a little prick of pain in her side. She looked down. He held an open knife against her, hiding it with his body. The point had already pierced her dress.

"My car is that old Morris, Mrs. Theobald. Don't make a fuss or try anything. Just get in. Get in at the driver's door, then slide along to the passenger seat."

"Let me go," she whispered. "What's it all about? Let me go."

She felt almost paralysed with fear. Her step stumbled.

"Get into the car, Mrs. Theobald."

When she hesitated, she felt again the point of the knife.

"I'm desperate," he muttered, close to her ear. "Do as I say. Get in."

She got in.

As she slid across to the passenger seat, she wildly contemplated thrusting open the far door and running for it. But he was too quick. Already he was in the driving seat, ramming at the starter with his foot, keeping a grip on her arm.

The engine stuttered, then roared. He drove quickly through the car park, down the Gorsedene entrance road.

"Keep quiet, Mrs. Theobald, and don't try anything. I still have a knife ready. I could use it without stopping the car."

She saw that the knife lay open on his lap. If she tried to grab it, he'd have it up before she could reach it. Anyway, she was too terrified to make the attempt; too terrified to say anything.

Lal was driving madly fast. As they neared the Gorsedene entrance gates, she saw the Neals hastily stepping on to the grass verge to get out of the way.

Had they seen her? She could not be sure.

The car was out on the road now, Lal accelerating, taking it as fast as it would go; much too fast for thinking of flicking open the door and jumping.

She thought she might try that at the traffic lights this side of the town, and prayed they would be red. When they came to the lights, they were red. But Lal drove straight across them, swerving just to miss a car cutting in front of him, the driver of that car startled, cursing, shouting.

Then Lal turned sharply on to a minor country road. There would be no more traffic lights.

CHAPTER 15

WHEN HE HAD lunched, Henry went to his bedroom to work on his briefs. He kept at it for an hour, but then admitted that his attention was wandering, he was wasting his time.

What distracted him was the nagging anxiety that Kate would go to the police with her wild theories. If it had been anybody else, that would not have mattered. The police would have made a polite note of what she said, and left it at that.

But with Kate it would matter a great deal. He knew exactly what use Kate would make of the situation. She would phone a story to the *Post*, declaring that, in spite of the inquest verdict on Philip Antrobus, the police were considering the possibility that he was murdered. The *Post* would splash the story next morning. Because of the repercussions of the collapse of Antrobus Enterprises, that story would go all round the world. Heaven knew what the consequences might be.

So he put aside his work and drove to Gorsedene.

The girls at the reception desk telephoned Kate's room, but there was no answer. "I think I saw Mrs. Theobald setting out for a walk," she told Henry.

He went on to the terrace to wait for her. The Gorsedene patients were slowly assembling for the cups of tea. A body emerged from the house with the first laden tray.

Michael and Mary Neal came out on the terrace.

"Hallo, there," said Michael. "Have you come to tea?"

"I'm waiting for Kate. But I'd like a cup of tea."

"Won't you join us? Kate went for a walk along the river bank. She'll be back soon, I guess."

"That's what she said she was going to do," put in Mary Neal, "but I don't think she did."

"I'm sure you were mistaken, my dear."

Henry was looking puzzled.

"We went for a walk down the entrance road as far as the Gorsedene gates,' Michael explained. "As we were turning to come back, Charan Lal, the Indian porter here, came down the road in his old jalopy, going much too fast. He's an erratic driver, I assure you, from experience. A few days ago he took Mary and me on a trip around the countryside. It was a mite hair-raising.

"Anyway, we stepped on to the grass to let him pass. There was a woman in the car with him. Mary thought she was Kate."

The boy came up with the tray of tea, serving them.

"Today," said Michael, smiling happily, "we get biscuits —wholemeal, of course, and cooked from stoneground wheaten flour flavoured with blackstrap molasses. Deelicious." To the boy he added, "Is it Charan's afternoon off?"

"No, sir. He's supposed to be doing the teas, but nobody can find him. They called me in from weeding in the kitchen garden."

When he had gone, Mary said, "There you are. Charan has gone off somewhere, and I'm nearly sure it was Kate in the car with him."

"Well, maybe," her husband conceded. "He could have offered to show her round the countryside, as he offered us."

"When he's supposed to be on duty? It all seems to me odd."

"I shouldn't worry," Henry assured her. "Kate gets hunches from time to time and goes dashing off in pursuit of wild geese."

"Like all good newspaper persons," agreed Michael, smiling.

"She probably asked the porter to drive her somewhere or other—if it really was Kate with him," said Henry.

But after the Neals had gone to their room, excusing themselves because they were in the middle of packing,

Mary's doubts began to infect Henry. There was still no sign of Kate. He considered setting off along the river bank to meet her. But he might easily miss her, for she could have turned back through the woods, say, as she had before.

A small doubt nagged. So he walked round to the car park. If she had gone with Lal, somebody might have seen her.

There was nobody in the car park. He went on into the stable yard. Two men were hoisting sacks of feed into the loft above the stalls.

Henry spoke to the man on the ground. "Did you by any chance notice Mr. Lal, the Indian porter, drive off with a lady about an hour ago?"

"Don't know whether he drove off with her, sir. But Charan was talking to the lady who asked about the block and tackle."

"Block and tackle?" asked Henry.

He felt a sudden tremor in his stomach.

"That's it, sir. The lady was asking about the block and tackle that got stolen—last Monday, wasn't it, Fred? Yes, last Monday. The one Charan found in the woods and brought back, couple of days later."

Henry, forcing himself to be calm, asked, "How did the conversation arise?"

"Well, sir, the lady was passing, and she commented on the block and tackle being useful for lifting heavy weights, and noticed we had a new one. So I told her about the old one being pinched, and Lal bringing it back. He happened to be passing, so I called over to ask him where he found it, in the woods, wasn't it? And he said, that's right, in the woods. That's about all. They both went on."

Henry could see that the man was puzzled at the interrogation. But he had to persist.

"Which way did they go?"

The man was staring at him. "Through the car park, I think. Was it through the car park the lady went, Fred? Yes, that's right, sir. And Lal went that way, too."

"Do you happen to know what car Mr. Lal drives?"

The stable hand grinned. "If you can call it a car. It's an old Morris—very old. Marvel it still runs."

"Thank you," said Henry, making for the car park, the stable hand looking after him with some bewilderment.

There was no elderly Morris parked among the Rolls and Bentleys.

Henry hurried round to the front entrance of the house and asked the reception girl if Mr. Neal was in his room. She phoned, and nodded.

"Please tell him Mr. Theobald is coming up to see him," said Henry, moving towards the stairs.

He was certain now that he needed help. And Michael Neal was the most likely man to know where the Indian might be.

2

The car was skirting the little town, Kate realized, and making along a lonely side-road for the woods beyond.

After a few minutes, Lal pulled off into the small, unkempt yard of an ancient-looking cottage. Immediately the car stopped he was out of his seat, round to the near side door, taking Kate's arm and helping her out.

"We will go into the cottage, please, Mrs. Theobald. If you do as you are told, you will not be harmed in any way."

Kate wondered whether she could shake him off and run for it; but realized it was hopeless. She did not know where she was, or where she could run, and she fancied Lal could outpace her easily.

As though he knew what she was thinking, he said, "There is no other house for a quarter of a mile. If you shout or scream, you will not be heard. Now, go into the cottage, please."

The other Indian was seated in the shabby, sparsely-furnished room. There was no sign of the girl. As she entered, Lal spoke rapidly to the other in their own tongue. The man looked startled, but Lal was obviously reassuring him.

Turning to Kate, he said, "It will be necessary for you to stay here for a couple of days, Mrs. Theobald. But no harm will come to you."

"You won't get away with it, Charan; not with murder."

"I have committed no murder."

"Come on," she said. "I know that Philip Antrobus was garrotted in his bedroom, then hanged from that pipe to make it look like suicide. What I could not understand, and what my husband said nullified the whole thing, was how anyone could have lifted him single-handed and got the cord round his neck and the pipe. Henry—that's my husband—reckoned it was physically so difficult as to be almost impossible. But when I found out about that block and tackle..."

She waited for him to say something, but he remained silent, watching her solemnly.

So she went on, "I know you could get into that room with a pass key. I know your motive—the sufferings of your family among workers on the Antrobus tea plantations in Assam, where you yourself led the riot that failed. Don't think I'm unsympathetic. You certainly had some sort of moral right to retribution. But not to murder."

"Murder was not our plan," he replied. "Antrobus's death was not what we wanted. We intended to kidnap him, that is all. This old cottage has a cellar where we meant to hold him."

"You must have been crazy to imagine that kidnapping him would have solved anything. Whatever you extracted from him, he could nullify when he got free. You did not mean to kidnap him, Charan. You meant to murder him as vengeance."

"You do not know everything, Mrs. Theobald. I believe you do not know that we were seeking to solve our problems by peaceful means. I had got together a group of business men in Bombay, backed by one of our banks, to offer to buy the plantations from Antrobus Enterprises, and run them as a co-operative. Antrobus was willing to sell. Everything was arranged. The contract was drawn up. Then suddenly he refused to sign unless we increased our offer to an impossibly high figure. So then I had the contract sent to me in England, and I and my friends planned to kidnap Antrobus and force him to sign."

"Force him?"

"He would have signed. I do not think Antrobus was a very brave man, or would have suffered much pain for very long. I think he would have signed after just a few hours."

"Now I know you're mad," she protested. "No contract could be enforced that had been signed under duress."

Lal shook his head. "I am not mad, Mrs. Theobald. Also, I am a student of law. The tea company which Antrobus bought from an Indian concern is registered, not in England, but in India. I do not think that Antrobus would have had much success in seeking to annul that contract in Calcutta courts. Feeling about the tea plantations runs high out there. I doubt if he would even have tried. He would have taken what is a fair price for his company, and let it go."

A calculated risk, Kate saw. It might even have come off—except for the kidnap hunt that would have started.

"You'd never have got away," she told him, "if Antrobus was missing."

"We have our escape route planned, Mrs. Theobald. My friend here and I have the air tickets, and an understanding with a certain airline that we can leave at any time."

"For India? They'd have to extradite you."

"Not for India. There are places in the world that do not consider acts of political justice to be crimes. Libya, for one example. Syria for another. When we were somewhere safe, there is a girl who is not known to be one of us. You saw her in the woods that afternoon, which a little alarmed us. She would telephone the police to let them know where Antrobus could be found—here in the cellar. He would have been hungry for only two days. Just like Gorsedene, Mrs. Theobald," he added with a slow smile.

"Then why did you kill him?"

"I would prefer him not to be dead. But it does not matter very much. Now that he is dead, his executors will surely complete the contract for the tea plantations, so our objective will be achieved. And, as a matter of fact, I did not kill him."

"Oh bosh. The block and tackle."

"I will tell you what happened," he said slowly. "It does not matter, because my friend and I will leave tonight, when the girl will telephone the police to say where you are." He smiled. "We will leave you food and drink, unless you prefer to complete your health treatment."

"You said you'd tell me what happened."

"Why not? That evening we planned to kidnap Antrobus. I had learned that he might leave Gorsedene next day. It was as part of our plan to kidnap him, of course, that I took a college-vacation job as porter there.

"So that evening we met in the woods—the girl as well —in readiness to abduct him. That was when we saw what happened to the helicopter pilot."

"To Charles Pugh?" she asked, astonished.

"Yes, I remember, that was his name. He was sitting on a tree trunk by the side of a fire-safety lane through the trees. It happened to be near where we were meeting. We feared for a while that he would interfere with our plan. It was a question of timing. He seemed to be waiting for somebody. We lay under cover, and kept quiet, anxious in case he did not go away in time.

"But then a car drove along the fire lane and Mr. Sherwood got out to talk to Mr. Pugh. He was offering him a large sum of money, which he had in an attache case, for some papers—I do not know what the papers were."

"I do," said Kate. "Go on."

"Mr. Pugh was very angry, in a great rage. He hit Mr. Sherwood, knocking him back against his car. Mr. Sherwood wrenched open the lid of the boot and picked up a big spanner to defend himself. As Mr. Pugh ran at him, Mr. Sherwood struck him on the forehead, very hard. I do not think he meant to kill him. After a little while, when Mr. Pugh did not move, and there was blood flowing on the pathway, Mr. Sherwood saw what he had done. He picked Mr. Pugh up and put him into the boot of his car. Then he drove off. I suppose he put him in that quarry where his body was found this morning."

"And you did not stop him?"

Lal shrugged. "What should I care about an Englishman —any Englishman? And we had other business. We were already a little late with our plan. I was to go into Antrobus's room, to gag and tie him. The two others were outside, at places I had chosen, to signal to me when the way was clear down the service stairway and across to the car park, where I had my car."

"And in the struggle with Philip Antrobus you strangled him," said Kate.

"No, Mrs. Theobald. When I let myself into his room, I found him lying on the floor, already dead. He had been strangled. Beside him was a long silken thong with a little leather handle, a sort of whip. He had been strangled with that.

"I was about to leave, without touching anything when the room door began to open. I slipped back into the bathroom, which was in darkness. So I could see the person who entered the room, carrying that block and tackle."

"Who?"

"Mr. Dimpsey."

3

Henry hurried up the stairs to the Neals' room. They were packing clothes into two grips open on the bed.

"Sorry to interrupt you, but I think Kate was in that car with the Indian, and that he has taken her off forcibly."

Michael was incredulous. "Charan kidnapped her? Why the devil should he?"

"It's too complicated to explain now. I think Kate has discovered that he was implicated in some way in Philip Antrobus's death, and he knows that she has."

"You can't mean that Kate's crazy idea that Antrobus was murdered . . . "

"I don't know. But I'm not risking anything. Kate said you had got to know this man Lal. Have you any idea where he might have taken her?"

"He and another Indian student are staying at an old cottage they've rented, out in the country on the far side of the town. I think maybe I could find it again."

"Will you come with me?"

"Sure."

"Me too," said Mary.

"No," Henry told her. "Stay here. We may need somebody to communicate with—to alert the police, maybe."

Michael was into his jacket. "Kidnapping? It's fantastic."

"Come on."

His car was in the park. They took the road towards the town, Michael trying to recall the route to the cottage; past the traffic lights, then about half a mile farther there was a side turning . . . He was a little uncertain because when Charan stopped off at the cottage on the outing with Mary and himself, they had been returning to Gorsedene. He had to work out the route in reverse, in his memory.

But once they were across the lights he spotted the side road.

Henry turned into it. "How far to the cottage?"

Michael thought it was only a few minutes' drive. In fact he did not place it until they had driven past and he looked back.

Henry drove on for half a mile, turned the car in a farm gateway and came slowly back. Some distance short of the cottage he flicked out the gear and let the car coast as far as it would in silence.

"Isn't that a little dramatic?" asked Michael, but nevertheless keeping his voice down.

"If I'm wrong, it doesn't matter. If I'm right, we'd better take precautions. On his record in Assam, the man's a terrorist."

They found a footpath leading towards the back of the cottage.

When he saw Lal's car in the yard, Henry touched Michael's arm and told him to stay under cover. Then he moved quietly forward and looked into the car. A woman's handbag lay on the floor by the side of the front passenger seat. He recognized it as Kate's.

He crept back across the yard to the hedge where Michael was crouching.

"She's in there," he whispered. "Her handbag's on the floor of the car."

"What do we do? Call the cops?"

"Too risky. They may be armed. We'd simply create a hostage situation, with Kate as hostage."

"So?"

"So we go in and get her. Agree?"

"Sure."

"Then move quietly," said Henry. "We're not at much risk of being seen in this dusk." He pointed to a ground-floor window through which a light was dimly showing. "Let's find out first what we can see inside."

They went carefully across the yard, Henry leading. He flattened against the wall beside the lit window, then edged forward. It was meagrely curtained. Through a chink he could see about half the room. There was a bare wooden table with a meal on it. Charan Lal was seated at the table, eating. Now and then he looked across and spoke to somebody just out of vision.

Henry leaned back and whispered to Michael, "I can see Lal. He's seated at the table, eating. There's somebody else, but I can't see who. Let's try the door."

It had a simple latch. Henry eased it and the door gently gave.

"We'll go in fast," he whispered. "If there's any reaching for weapons, don't wait. Rush them. I'll take Lal. You take whoever he's talking to, unless of course it's Kate. But we don't want a fight unless it's forced on us."

"Okay. Say when."

"Now," said Henry, shoving the door.

It opened directly into the room, cottage fashion. Opposite Lal was seated another Indian, also eating. It was a dish of rice, smelling savoury.

Both men looked towards the door as Henry and Michael stepped swiftly into the room, halting close enough to the Indians to lunge if need be. But neither made any aggressive movement.

"Where is my wife?" demanded Henry.

"How should I know, Mr. Theobald?" asked Lal.

"Come now, Charan," Michael expostulated, "Mary and I were at the Gorsedene entrance and we saw you driving off with Mrs. Theobald beside you."

"Yes of course. I was coming from the park when she stopped me and asked if I would drive her into town. She wanted to find you, Mr. Theobald. I said I was passing a couple of blocks away from the Crown, and she said that would do fine. So I set her down at the traffic lights, sir. Did she not find you?"

Henry said curtly, "You're lying. Her handbag is in your car. Where is she?"

The other man suddenly gabbled a few sentences to Lal in their own language.

"Now," cried Henry sharply.

He flung himself at Lal, overturning him in his chair, pinning his arms.

At the same moment Michael went for the other Indian. But he was farther off. Before Michael could get a grip on him, he flicked a knife, stabbing sharply at one of Michael's arms and, as he recoiled, catching the other and twisting it behind his back.

From where he held Lal on the floor, Henry turned his head and saw that the other Indian was holding the knife close to Michael's face.

"Let Lal go," said the man in whining English, "or your friend is hurt."

"Hang on to him, Henry," urged Michael thickly.

But his face was white, blood was already staining through the coatsleeve of his wounded arm.

The Indian made a small cut in Michael's cheek; he could not help but flinch.

"Let him go," the Indian ordered, "or next time it's his eye."

There was nothing for it. Henry released his hold on Lal and let him up from the floor.

The two Indians spoke briefly in their own tongue. Then Lal went quickly from the cottage. The other still held Michael at knife point.

There was the sound of a car starting.

The Indian shoved Michael aside and ran for the door.

By the time Henry had helped Michael up, then followed, the car had gone. The yard was empty, except that in the light from the doorway he could see Kate's handbag, the contents spilled on the ground where it had been flung from the departing car.

4

When he returned to the room, Michael had gone. A far door was open.

Through it, Michael called, "There's only a small kitchen here. Try upstairs."

Henry grunted and made for the cottage stairs. There were two small upper rooms. They were empty. He saw a trapdoor into a loft, piled a chair on a rickety bed and scrambled on, hauling himself up, shoving the trap. The loft was tiny. It contained nothing.

He hurried back downstairs. Michael had slumped on to a kitchen chair. He was holding his handkerchief to his cheek.

"Don't bother with me," he said weakly. "Find Kate."

Henry said nothing. He eased off Michael's jacket, found a kitchen knife to split the sleeve of his shirt, revealing the wound—nasty, but only surface.

"You'll be all right," he said. With the knife he cut off the shirt sleeve, improvising a bandage, tying it tightly, stanching the blood. "How about your face?"

"I've cut myself worse shaving. Find Kate."

Henry stood there, uncertain. Where else to look? Maybe there was an outhouse. He had no torch but could feel about in the dark.

They both heard the front door of the cottage open and shut; and footsteps.

She came into the kitchen—the Indian girl. When she saw them, she halted in dismay, then turned to run. But Henry was too fast for her. Before she could reach the cottage door, he had caught her by the arm, swung her round, pulled her back into the kitchen.

"Now then, where's my wife?"

"How would I know? I do not even know who is your wife. Where is Charan? What are you doing here?"

Henry shook her. "Where is she?"

The girl was silent.

"Listen, please," Michael intervened in a placatory voice. "This is Mr. Theobald, a lawyer. His wife is Kate Theobald, the journalist who was staying at Gorsedene and who reported Philip Antrobus's death in the *Daily Post*. For some reason that I do not know, Charan Lal took her away in his car and brought her here. But we cannot find her."

"Where is Charan?" the girl repeated.

"He and his friend have made a run for it in his car," Henry told her, "leaving you to carry the can."

"What can? I have done nothing."

"We'll take your word for that," Michael assured her. "Myself, I've simply no idea what's been going on. But whatever, it must be much worse if Mrs. Theobald has been hurt, or held prisoner. We have searched this house, and she is not here."

"Have you searched the cellar?"

"The cellar?" he asked, surprised. "Where's the way down?"

For the first time the girl smiled. "You are sitting on it."

Michael looked down, puzzled.

"Under the mat," she said.

He got up, shifted his chair and with his good arm tugged away the floor mat. The stone slab beneath was fitted with an old iron ring.

"Watch the girl," said Henry.

He seized the ring, but had to use all his strength to lift the slab and slide it clear of the opening.

A flight of wooden steps led down to a dimly-lit cellar. At their foot stood Kate.

"Gracious, it's you, Henry. I didn't know what the devil was going on—all that banging about up there. If I'd known it was you, I'd have shouted."

He leaned down to help her up. "Are you all right?"

"Yes, perfectly." She saw the girl, and Michael. "What's happening? Where's Charan and his pal?"

"They scooted in his car," Henry told her. "We tried to stop them, but the other one had a knife."

She saw that Michael was bandaged. "Are you badly hurt?"

"Nothing to worry about," he assured her cheerfully.

Henry pushed Kate on to the chair. "Take it easy now. And tell me what happened. Why did he kidnap you?"

"The three of them planned to seize Philip Antrobus on Monday evening, bring him here and torture him until he signed a contract selling the tea plantations to a co-operative in Bombay."

"They must have been mad. That doesn't make sense."

"Better sense than you'd think," she said. "But it's complicated. I'll tell you later. What matters is that Charan in fact got into Antrobus's room to grab him, but found him already dead. That's what he says."

"You believe him?"

"Yes, I think so. Anyway, this afternoon he found me nosing about in something that might get him involved."

"The block and tackle?" asked Henry.

"You know about that?" she asked, surprised.

"I talked to the stable hand. Explain later."

"So Charan panicked. He has a record of terrorism in India. Maybe he could have been got at here . . . "

"Conspiracy, possibly."

"He'd have known that. He's reading law. Anyway, he panicked, forced me into his car with a knife and brought me here. I was to stay in the cellar until he and his pal got away by air to some country that harbours terrorists. Which is it?" she asked the girl. "Syria? Libya?"

The girl stared at her with contempt.

"They'll be on their way now," Henry considered. "We'd better get to the police fast if they're to be stopped at the airport. Bound to be either Heathrow or Gatwick."

"There's something much more important," Kate said. "They all saw what happened to Charles Pugh. Sherwood killed him." She raised a hand to check questions from Henry, startled exclamations from Michael. Then narrated what Charan Lal had told her of the fight in the woods.

She stood up and faced the girl. "Listen. I bear absolutely no malice against Charan. On one condition, I'll not say anything to the police about being brought here by force."

"Now, wait a minute," Henry protested.

"What's the point, Henry? Charan never intended to do

me any harm. It was simply that he panicked." She turned to the girl. "I'll go further. I think that what you tried to do was morally justified. I hope that the scheme succeeds. I won't do anything to hinder it. I probably won't let it be known that Charan was in Philip Antrobus's room that night, but that's not a promise. It depends on a couple of checks I have to make."

"What is your condition?" asked the girl.

"That you testify about the fight you saw in the woods, when Sherwood killed Charles Pugh."

The girl made no reply.

"Ah well," said Kate, "she'll talk when the police question her. After all, witness to murder . . . "

"Manslaughter," corrected Henry.

"Okay. Either will fix Sherwood. You can have that typescript, Michael. Find your Scotland Yard man as soon as you can, Henry."

"My car's down the road."

"Take the girl," Kate instructed. "I expect they'll be in time to stop the two Indians at the airport. But if not, there's still the girl. She saw what happened. Get her to the Super fast. And I meant it about not squealing on Charan Lal. You're not to say anything about his bringing me here forcibly."

"What about the block and tackle?"

"I'm not sure that it really means anything."

"Charon Lal thought it did. That's why he grabbed you."

"No, I don't think so," Kate said calmly. "He has such a sharp intelligence that he understood what I suspected. I could well have been wrong—just my own crazy idea. But if I took the story of the block and tackle to the police, it would involve him anyway, since he brought the gear back. He'd be linked with the Assam riots; he knew from talking with Michael that I was aware of his part in those. So he made a spot decision to get away by the planned escape route—and he had to keep me quiet until he was safely hidden. That's all. It simply doesn't matter, compared with telling the police about Pugh."

As they moved towards the cottage door, Kate said, "But I am rather whacked. Quite an evening on only raw-vegetable salad. Drop me off at Gorsedene, Henry, so that I can go to bed. Tell the Super I'll co-operate fully in the morning. Come on, we're wasting time."

As they left the cottage she squealed with delight.

"My handbag!"

She ran to pick up the scattered contents.

"You'll have to give me a few minutes. I haven't done anything about cosmetics for hours. I must look terrible."

CHAPTER 16

THERE WAS nobody in the entrance hall at Gorsedene.

"You come in, too, Michael," Kate suggested. "No point in letting the police see your arm. They'd be inquisitive. Anyway, you ought to have it dressed."

"Mary can do that. She trained as a nurse."

"Good."

Out of the car, Kate opened the doors and slipped on the children's safety locks.

The Indian girl watched her with indifference. "You need not worry, Mrs. Theobald. I have no intention of trying to run. I have done nothing, and so I have no need to fear facing the police."

"Just a precaution," said Kate cheerfully.

"And they will not catch Charan," the girl told her as Henry prepared to move off. "They are not so stupid as to have chosen an obvious route. By midnight they will be out of England, and by tomorrow night in safety."

"I meant it when I said I'd keep absolutely quiet about Charan, if you'll testify to the police about the fight in the woods."

The girl shrugged. "Why not? I saw it happen."

"And did not report it," murmured Henry.

She smiled. "I am a foreigner, on a visit from a far country. I know nothing of your English laws."

Henry chuckled. "You'd not get away with that. But they'll need you as a witness. Just say you were too frightened to go to the police, until you met us tonight, and we persuaded you that you must. They'll accept that."

"It won't be too bad," Kate assured her. "Once you've put them on the right track, they'll find plenty of corroborative evidence. Blood marks in the boot of Sherwood's car, probably. Blood in the soil where he was knocked down. You can take the police to the right place. The forensic chaps will do the rest."

"And it's quite likely," Henry added, "that the post mortem will show that some of the contusions on the body that were caused when it pitched into that quarry were made after death."

He engaged the gear and moved away.

Kate and Michael entered the house. At her room, Kate gave him the typescript and the photostats. He murmured his gratitude.

"Now get along to Mary and have that wound dressed. And Michael, please keep quiet about this evening. Not a word to anyone. Promise?"

He promised with a smile. "Anyhow, I wouldn't know what to say. The fact is, I'm itching with curiosity."

"I'm not scratching."

"Okay. But I'm to be in London in a couple of months for a conference. Meet me. I'll call you at the *Post*. I've simply got to know the rest."

"Some of it, maybe."

When he had gone she tried the phone. No answer. Nobody on the switchboard, of course. So she went down to the booth in the entrance hall and dialled her newspaper, and put over the fact that Charles Pugh's death was being treated by the police as murder, and they expected to make an arrest shortly.

She was switched to Butch. "What gives, Kate?"

"I've said all I can at the moment. For your information, it'll probably turn out to be manslaughter—and the man they're after is John Sherwood."

Butch whistled softly.

"I'm going home tomorrow. I'll call you at your home," she went on. "I don't want to follow this one up, Butch. Will you put somebody else on it, please?"

"Okay. Call me. Will you have anything else by Sunday?"

"I don't know. Maybe."

She hung up and stepped back into the hall. Still nobody around. She went out on to the terrace. There was a light in the front window of the director's cottage. After a moment of hesitation, she walked down the drive towards it.

From the road she could see Pelham Dimpsey, seated at his desk, staring at something that lay on it.

She knocked at the front door. Pelham himself opened to her. He did not seem surprised. He said nothing.

"May I come in?" she asked. "I've been talking to Charan Lal."

"I know. Half an hour ago he telephoned to tell me."

He turned without saying more, leading the way into his front room, himself resuming the seat at his desk.

2

"Charan says you killed Philip Antrobus."

Pelham Dimpsey said nothing.

He had discarded his white overall, of course, and was dressed in a trim grey suit. He seemed as immaculate as ever. But there was a look in his face that, for some reason Kate could not name, was frightening. He was sitting quite still, except for the white hands with the hair thick on the knuckles. They were slightly tremulous.

Since he was evidently not going to speak, Kate went on, "I think you probably know that Charan planned to kidnap Philip Antrobus on that Monday evening, and why. I know that, when I entered the room, Antrobus was lying dead on the floor, strangled with a silken thong. That would be, I suppose, at about half past nine.

"I know that you returned to the room, carrying the block and tackle you had taken from the stables. Charan hid in the bathroom, then emerged. You must almost have dropped with shock."

The man was staring in her direction, but Kate had the odd impression that his eyes were sightless, that he was not seeing her.

Then suddenly he focused, and spoke. "I told you that Lal telephoned to me half an hour ago. He wanted to warn me that he had told you a lot of fanciful lies, because he thought you might involve him in the Antrobus matter, and he was afraid."

"I don't think they were lies," Kate answered. "I believe

it is true that Charan helped you to string the body to that bathroom pipe. With the two of you, you did not really need the block and tackle after all. You got him to dispose of it afterwards, and pretend that a couple of days later he found it in the woods. I don't know what happened to that silken whipcord. I expect you took it away and burned it."

After a pause, she continued, "I wondered at first why ever Charan should have agreed to help you to cover up murder. Then I realized that the question should rather be, why should he not? With his record in Assam, he had no wish to get involved in Antrobus's death in any way. If it could be passed off as suicide, that would suit Charan fine. Did you ever wonder whether he might blackmail you later? But no. He's not that kind of man."

Dimpsey stirred, and focused his gaze on her again. "There is no truth in what you are saying."

"I know it was not quite like that," she assented. "But I think I know, near enough, what really happened. Would you like to tell me? All right, let me tell you. The way I see it is this. You knew that your old friend Philip was vicious in a certain way—he was a flagellant. But I think you did not know, until Monday night, that your wife, who had known him so long, had all that time been his mistress and shared, or at least suffered, his vice. All those visits to London recently; you didn't suspect then, but now you know what they were for. You'll say I'm guessing. But I don't think I'm wrong. That whip, lying by his body, is conclusive."

Kate paused. But, knowing that he would not speak, waited for only a short time.

"Janet went to his room on Monday evening at about half past eight. Bella was there, so your wife made some excuse of a business message from you. When Bella had gone, the erotic play began. From the next room I vaguely remember hearing laughter. His laughter, I suppose."

She saw that the man winced a little at that, and moved his hands on the desk.

"I was half asleep, remember," she went on. "Some time later, about half an hour later, I think I heard a curious tapping noise. The strokes of a silken whip?"

She saw his hands tauten where they lay on the desk; the knuckles, dark with hair, gripping the nails into the palms.

"Then I heard a thud. I'm still guessing, remember. She hated him. I don't know why, but she must have hated him. Perhaps the whip happened to coil round his neck as he crouched on the bed, naked, more than half drunk. Perhaps it was part of the game that a silken cord round the neck was a pretence of threat.

"On impulse, she grabbed the cord, pulled at it, tightened it sharply round his throat and held on until his body rolled off the bed and fell to the floor with a thud.

"Then she ran. Only half-dressed, maybe. She ran to you. I won't try to imagine what she said, what she confessed.

"Horrified, desperate, you hastened to his room, found him dead, realized you could make it seem suicide if you could string him to the pipe in the bathroom by his gown cord. Impossible—until you thought of the block and tackle, and hurried to the stable to fetch it.

"And returned to find Charan. Did he help you to get the pyjamas back on the man's body, and thrust his arms into the dressing-gown itself? A gruesome thing. Was that worst of all?"

Dimpsey said nothing. But he was staring at her now with attention.

"You can be calm about Charan," she said. "I know that I probably cannot substantiate any of this by means of Charan Lal. He has gone, and I doubt if he will be found."

When Dimpsey spoke now, his voice was hoarse. "You have a distraught imagination, Mrs. Theobald. Philip hanged himself."

Ignoring that, she asked, "Why did she hate him? Was he forcing her to do what he wanted by using some threat? Your position at Gorsedene? But that was finished anyway by his failure . . ."

Dimpsey handed her a piece of paper from his desk. It was a note written in a shaky hand on lined paper torn from a child's exercise book.

Darling.

He always threatened to tell you that Christopher was his child, not yours. I know how you love Christopher, so I submitted. What did it matter? My body has belonged to him for years anyway. What does anything matter?

Kate looked up. "Where is she?"

"A man walking his dog by the river two hours ago... No, she's not dead. He got her out in time. They have taken her to hospital. She has a complete breakdown. It has happened twice before. The doctor hinted, last time, that another breakdown could be permanent. I don't know."

"What will you do?"

"God knows. Leave here. Start somewhere else, in some other country. Wherever it is, I shall take them both with me—her and the boy. You cannot stop me. There is not one shred of evidence to substantiate one word of your fanciful guesswork. Philip hanged himself. Now go please, Mrs. Theobald."

3

At mid-morning on Saturday, Henry arrived in the car to drive Kate back to Chelsea. She had already eaten her last grapefruit, quaffed her last glass of boiled water, stood on the scale in the bath-house, been given a valedictory massage; she had nodded a farewell to Bella's topknot in the next cabinet, tipped the girls generously, marvelled slightly to herself that none of them knew anything of what had happened to Janet Dimpsey except that she had been taken ill; she had packed, paid the bill at the reception desk for her extras, exchanged politeness with the girl at the desk, and greeted Henry (who tipped the boy from the kitchen garden, standing in as porter, generously).

When they were on the road, away from the place, she asked, "Did that girl co-operate with the police?"

"About Sherwood? Yes. They took him in this morning from his London flat. He's helping them with their enquiries, as they say. It'll be manslaughter. But Stoddart is hugging himself about the fraud charge that will follow."

"How about Charan and his friend?"

"They got away. The girl was right. They took a night flight on a holiday package trip from Luton to Paris. Early this morning they flew on to Beirut, before the police got around to them. No further trace, but it sounds like Syria. I suppose they'll lie low for a bit, then surface quietly in India when it's all forgotten—unless you have something really convincing about that block and tackle."

"Oh no," she said. "Seems there was nothing in that. The block and tackle just went missing, and Charan happened to find it in the woods."

Henry took his eyes from the road for a quizzical look at her. "Which was why, I suppose, he locked you in a cellar, and then beat it for the Middle East."

"He lost his nerve, Henry. He thought I would involve him in the Antrobus affair, so he'd better run. And I had to be kept quiet until he was safely away. I was wrong about any significance to that block and tackle. You, as usual, were right—you and the coroner both."

Back in her flat, while Henry parked the car, Kate sighed contentedly, made herself a pot of strong coffee and opened her biscuit tin. With a couple of chocolate Bourbons and three cream crunches she settled by the phone and dialled Butch at home.

"Butch, I've got an absolutely sensational story. I'm coming in to the office tomorrow, to write it for Monday's paper."

"About Antrobus?"

"Antrobus? No, he hanged himself. Surely you read the inquest verdict. This is something that will interest far more of our readers than a story about a bust tycoon."

"Tell me."

"In only six days I lost nine pounds and six ounces. Fabulous!"

*It passed
from the dead
to the living,
a beautiful gift
with a frightening power—*

THE AMULET

A sweltering southern town... a mysterious necklace... a family's burning house... a doomed policeman... a jealous woman turned killer... a babysitter enraged at a crying child. Where did it come from? Who would it strike next? And why? The horror was unspeakable, the terror unstoppable, and the chain was unbroken...

A Novel of Pure Terror
by MICHAEL McDOWELL

 Avon / 40584 / $2.25

AMU 4-79